# BY MAGIC GRANTED

## BY MAGIC
## BOOK FOUR

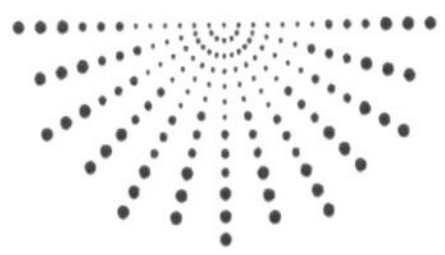

## MAGGIE SHAYNE

# CHAPTER ONE

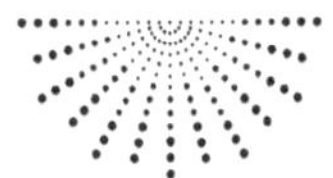

*The Wish*

Her tiny feet bare, her slippers dangling from two fingers, Enya tiptoed over the chilly stone floor to the arched window of her bedroom. A warm, sea-scented breeze kissed her face, lifted her hair and tugged at the gauzy thin silk of her dress. She inhaled deeply, a smile pulling at the corners of her mouth.

"You're going there again, aren't you?"

Enya stiffened, but relaxed almost immediately. It was only her older sister, Lena. She turned, leaning back against the stone sill, and fixed her face into an expression she hoped was all innocence. "I don't know what you're talking about, Lena. Goin' where?"

"Don't try to fool me with those big brown eyes, little

sister. You disappear every year when Haven Isle passes this way. Whenever we're in reach of that great mortal mainland where they wouldn't know a unicorn from a dragon. You go there. I know you do. You've been doing it for years."

Swallowing hard, Enya lifted her chin. "Don't be silly. It's forbidden to leave the isle. You know that." She realized that she was nervously fiddling with the miniature conch shell suspended from a cord around her neck and took her hand away.

"And so do you," her sister went on. "If Queen Ciarnan ever finds out what you've been up to—"

"She won't find out!" Enya hurried across the room, catching her sister's shoulders and holding them tightly. "Queen Ciarnan cannot know, Lena. She'd stop me from going anymore. I know she would. You won't tell, will you?"

Lena's blue eyes narrowed.

"Please," Enya said, and she touched the shiny black shell her sister wore, the one that matched her own. "Mother would have approved."

"That isn't fair," Lena said, but she sighed and lowered her head. "But I'll keep your secret.... *If* you'll tell me why you go there."

Enya relaxed, her shoulders slumping a bit. "I've always gone there, Lena. It's simple as that. From the time I learned to use my wings, I'd flit to the mortal world every year when our isle drifted within reach. It fascinates me." She let her hands fall to her sides, and paced slowly back to the window to stare out through the thin mist at the barely visible shape of a vast continent's coastline, deep purple on the horizon.

"There's more. I know there is."

Leaning her elbows on the stone windowsill, Enya stared at the world she longed to be a part of, but never could. The mortal world. "Yes. There's more. There's...there's a man." She heard her sister's sharp gasp and turned quickly. "It's not like *that*. I was only a girl the first time I saw him, and he a mere boy. But there was something about him..." Her eyes fell closed as Devon's beautiful face appeared in her mind's eye. His black satin hair, always wind-tossed and wild. The deep-sea blue of his eyes.

"This man has *seen* you? *Spoken* to you? Enya, how could you reveal us to a *mortal?* You've put us all in danger!"

"Oh, don't be foolish, Lena. He's no threat to us. He's sweet and gentle and..." She gave her head a shake. "And besides, he hasn't seen me, except in his dreams. I know the laws of secrecy as well as anyone. I only go to him when he's sleeping. Just so I can look at him, and smell his hair...and touch him."

*"Touch him?* Oh, Enya, this is bad. This is very bad. You shouldn't even be entering the mortal realm. You know it's deadly to pure-blood Fay of the royal line—"

"Sometimes," Enya said in a whisper. "When he was still a boy, I'd join him in his dreams, and we'd run and play together. But he grew up. He lost his belief in magic."

"That's just as well," Lena said, tossing her head. "You keep going there, you'll take ill."

"Nonsense. My short visits don't hurt. I once heard Queen Ciarnan say we could survive several days in mortal before we might suffer ill effects."

"All the same, Enya, you're breaking the rules. You'll be in terrible trouble should the queen ever learn—"

"Aye, but she won't, because you are going to keep my secret. You promised."

Lena nodded slowly. "But Enya 'tis said Queen Ciarnan knows everything that happens on this isle. She's bound to find out"

"Were she going to find out she'd have found out by now," Enya insisted. "And she obviously hasn't or she'd have done something about it." She hopped up onto the windowsill, and swung her legs over the edge. Before her the rolling green hills of the enchanted, floating island sloped downward to kiss the midnight blue sea.

Long ago, the legends said, two Fairy siblings, purebloods of the royal line, which were the only fairies with wings, created this island. It was enchanted and set adrift in the great sea so that their enemies, wizards and dark beings who would wipe them out and take all the magic for their own, would never find it. One of the sisters came made her home on isle, and took with her half of their kind. The other sister remained in the realm of Rush, where her offspring lived under constant threat from dark forces. Someone had to maintain the balance of light magic to dark, after all. But they could never risk the light being wiped out entirely. Hence, the existence of Haven Isle.

Far, far beyond the white-capped water lay the mortal world that had called to Enya all her life. She gave one last glance over her shoulder at her sister. "If anyone asks, I've but gone walking. All right?"

Lena hesitated, frowning, but nodded at last. "Oh, all right. But we must talk about this when you return."

Enya only smiled and pushed herself off the ledge. She let herself plummet nearly to the crystal cliffs below the castle, and heard her sister's squeak of alarm, before flexing her wings and catching an air current.

"Of all the mischievous fay-folk on this isle," her sister called after her, "I vow, Enya, you're the worst!"

Enya sent her sister a wink, and then fluttered away.

She rode the wind out over the ocean, frowning a bit at the dark clouds she saw gathering, and the deep rumble in the distant sky, and the nervous response of the sea below. But she cast off her concerns over the approaching storm when her wings took her into the night skies of the mortal world, and she flew faster, right to Devon's bedroom window.

It was not the same bedroom window he'd had as a boy. But the house was the same. A broad, white, motherly home, with a wide front porch that looked to Enya like a pair of open arms. Black shutters, and the rocky beach beyond them. A few hundred yards away stood the big, barnlike structure where Devon worked. He built sailing ships, her Devon did. He'd always loved the sea.

These days, Devon slept in the master bedroom, as he had since his father had died several years ago. Until recently, his brother Bryan had occupied the room across the hall. But she hadn't seen Bryan during her last couple of visits. She supposed he'd married and moved away.

It gave Enya a twinge of pain to think of Devon's brother leaving him. They'd been as close as any two people could be, for as long as she could remember.

Enya hovered outside Devon's bedroom window, peering through. But the tall four-poster bed lay empty and neat. And she didn't feel a hint of Devon's presence there.

The creak of a screen door drew her attention. Then voices, below. Someone on the porch. Enya flitted over there, and landed on the porch roof, peering over the edge to see the people below. Belle and George, who were technically employees, but, at the heart of it, were more like family. Belle had been far more than a housekeeper to Devon and Bryan. More like the mother they'd never known, Enya suspected as she tilted her head to listen.

"... never should have taken it out on a night like this," Belle was saying. She shook her head and stared worriedly at the white-capped sea not far away.

"Now, sweetie, no one can handle a sailboat like Devon can. He'll be fine."

"I'm not so sure about that Georgie, it seems to me he's asking for trouble, going out alone with this storm brewing. Seems to me he's...." Her voice trailed off as she shook her head.

"Tempting fate," George finished for her. "Still blaming' himself, I guess."

"We ought to call the Coast Guard," Belle said. "He should have been back by—"

Her words were cut off by a blinding flash of lightning, rapidly followed by a boom of thunder so sharp Enya felt it vibrate in the center of her chest. A gust of wind came charging off the sea, sending her hair out straight behind her. Enya faced the wind, staring out at the roiling ocean. Devon, alone in a sailboat in this?

She sprang from the rooftop, taking to the air with furious speed, closing her eyes and whispering her will to the fates. "Take me to Devon. Take me to him now." The wind lifted her and swept her along, and she let it, praying she wasn't too late.

Devon stood braced against the vicious wind, sea spray razing his cheeks, lightning ripping the sky apart overhead. He stood there, and he taunted it, dared it, faced it down. "You want me? Well, here I am," he shouted, his voice swallowed up by thunder. "Here I am, you bastard. Come and get me!"

Anyone looking at him would think him insane. But it wasn't madness that had driven him out there tonight. It was regret—regret so deep it ate at his soul, for a mistake that had proven far too costly.

The darkness was relieved only by the flashes of white

foam appearing and vanishing on the angry sea, and the increasingly frequent lightning strikes that left him blind and blinking. But he was used to darkness. There'd been very little other than darkness in his life for over a year now. He was angry with the sea and the skies and the fates. But he was even more angry at himself. He was not depressed or suicidal. He was furious and reckless and wild. "Come on," he taunted. "Come and get it!"

As if in answer, a monstrous wave of black water rose like a serpent in front of him. The way it paused for just a moment reminded Devon of a king cobra preparing to strike. He braced himself, and the wave swept down over him. He heard its roar, the splintering of wood, the tearing of fabric. He felt the chill of its icy embrace. And that was all.

There was an odd, floating sort of sensation. He felt as if his lower body was still in the water, but his upper half seemed to be floating above it. And he thought for a moment that his recklessness had got him killed, and that he was about to discover what really awaited him on the other side.

But then there was warm breath on his face, soft lips touching his cheek, and a hauntingly lovely voice, singing in a language he didn't know. It held a lilt that might have been Gaelic, and the resonance of a bell. And gradually he knew there were delicate arms encircling his chest from behind, pulling his body upward, skimming him through the sea at remarkable speed. Her hair snapped against his face. She was above him...as if she was *flying* or something.

And then his body was slipping over sand, farther and farther from the water, until he lay on a raised bit of beach where the waves didn't reach.

The woman knelt beside him, her small hands running over his face and through his hair, and her voice, still with that lilting magical accent, whispered, "Don't die, Devon MacKenzie. Don't ye dare."

He felt her lips covering his mouth then, and his starving lungs slowly filled with the sweetest air he'd ever inhaled. Her hair tickled his neck and his chest as she lifted her head away, only to lower it again a moment later, pressing those, succulent lips to his once more. And Devon thought it wouldn't have mattered if he'd been dead for a month, those lips would have brought him back.

She lifted her head away, and when she lowered it again this time, he slid his hands into her hair, and held her face to his, and he kissed her. Her sweetness filled him, and she didn't pull away. In fact, she kissed him back. God, she tasted good. But there was more. There was this sensation of warmth and...and *light*. Yes. Light, filling him right to his soul, where it had been dark for so long.

He didn't want to let her go. Not ever.

She sat up slowly. Devon forced his eyes open. He was dizzy, weak. His lungs ached, and his vision was blurry. But he hadn't thought himself delirious. Now, though, he wasn't so sure.

In the pale but growing light of the rising orange sun, he saw a woman too beautiful to be real...a woman he knew from somewhere. Soft sable and auburn curls, twisting and winding all the way to the sand on which she sat, and pooling there. Who knew how long it might be? Huge brown eyes like doe's eyes, slanting upward at the outer corners and making her look impish. Her eyes were deeper and more mysterious, and more heavily fringed, than any eyes he'd ever seen. And he knew those eyes. Her lips were as full as ripe plums, and every bit as sweet, and he knew them, too. She wore a powder-blue dress of something thin and sheer, and he could see her slender body beneath it. And for a long time her breasts held his attention. But then something moved behind her, and his gaze shifted, and he saw the all but transparent wings, and his heart tripped to a stop.

"You're all right," she whispered. It was Irish, her accent. "Don't be afraid."

"Are you ... an angel?"

Her smile was so bright and so lovely he wanted to kiss her again. Was it a sin, he wondered, to be over-whelmed with desire for an angel?

"No," she whispered. "I'm no angel. If you remembered me at all, you'd not be asking." A soft giggle, a gentle hand touching his face again, stroking him like a favorite pet. "I'm a fairy—though I'm not s'posed to be telling you so."

He blinked and looked at those wings again. "Are you real? Or am I dreaming?"

A sad expression overcame her. "Alas, I'm only a dream. Everybody in the mortal world knows there are no such things as fairies, don't they, Devon?"

She couldn't be real. No, of course not. She didn't exist, except in this odd, vivid dream. Still, she seemed so familiar. Her face...it was one he'd seen before, in other dreams. And it didn't hit his conscious mind until just then, but he'd dreamed of her often, on and off, when he'd been a small child. A younger version of her, but her all the same. For several years, going to sleep had been his favorite thing to do, because in his dreams, he could romp and play and get into mischief with her. His own, personal fairy. She'd been his best friend.

And now...just look at her, now.

A damned shame he'd outgrown those silly dreams. Or...he'd thought he had.

"If you're only a dream," he told her, lifting a hand to cup her cheek, "then there's no harm in my kissing you again."

"No," she said softly. "No, I can't see that there is." She let him pull her closer this time, until her body laid atop his, and her small breasts pressed tight to his chest. She was light as a feather, and full of fire. He wrapped his arms around her waist, and felt the touch of those mystical wings against the backs of his hands. He kissed her deeply, parting her lips with his, tracing their shape, tasting her. Wanting her. Needing her. It was a sensation like nothing he'd ever felt before. Not just physical desire. This was a hunger of the soul. A hunger he tried to assuage by feasting on the drugging nectar of her kiss.

And then, very gradually, he felt himself fading, slipping into an unnaturally deep sleep.

~

Enya lifted herself from the man's wet body, taking her lips away from his, though it broke her heart to do so. She sat for only a moment, knowing she had to leave right away, before he became lucid and realized she wasn't a figment of his imagination. But leaving him was the last thing in the world she wanted to do.

She gazed down at him, stroked his beautiful raven hair and his lovely face. A single tear fell from her eye, to land right there on his cheek. There had been a sadness lingering in Devon's eyes. A deep hurt. He was haunted, and she had no idea why.

"I do believe I love you, Devon MacKenzie," she whispered. "And my only wish... my only wish is that I might have you for my own. I could heal those wounds you're hidin' inside. I'd give anything... anything at all if only I could do that for you."

But it was a foolish wish, she knew. As a pureblood fairy, she couldn't survive long in his world. It simply wasn't to be. She kissed his mouth once more, and then she flitted away, back to the enchanted isle where she belonged. But she'd never be happy there. Never.

# CHAPTER TWO

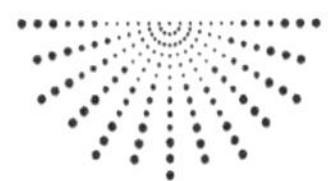

*The Risk*

The tap on his bedroom door was followed by Belle bustling through it, laden tray in hand. Devon smelled homemade biscuits and melting butter as he yanked a sheet over himself and sat up in bed.

"Belle, you didn't have to do that. I told you, I'm fine."

"I'll be the judge of that. Washed up on the beach like so much seaweed, barely conscious when we found you. That's far from fine, boy. If you were in better shape, I'd tan your hide for foolishness."

She settled the tray on his lap, and stood back, hands propped on ample hips, eagle eyes narrowed. She wouldn't leave until he ate, so he figured he might as well take a stab at it. He wasn't hungry in the least. Not for food, anyway. The soul-deep longing that gnawed at him was for the mysterious woman he'd dreamed about. The one he'd held tight to him for all too short a time, the one he'd kissed as if there would be no tomorrow.

It had seemed so real.

Real. Right. A real live fairy right there on the coast of Maine. And pigs could fly, too. But she was one hell of a hallucination. He'd gone to sleep last night eagerly, hoping against hope he'd dream of her again. But it hadn't happened. He'd awoken this morning feeling even emptier than he had before. And that was saying something. Those eyes. They still lingered vividly in his mind. So deep and brown and big and filled with...with wonder or magic or something.

"You're looking awfully pale, Devon. Are you sure you're feeling all right?"

He blinked twice, shook himself, and glanced up at Belle. "Fine. Really, Belle, I'm just fine." Dutifully, he picked up a still-warm biscuit and bit off a healthy portion.

Only then did Belle nod in approval and leave him in peace. And the second she closed the door, Devon got out of bed and pulled on some clothes. He gave Belle five minutes for good measure, before he slipped into the hallway, walking softly. He headed down the stairs and paused at the bottom. Pots and pans rattled from the kitchen. The coast was clear. He hurried across the foyer and out the front door, and he never slowed his pace until he was on the beach with the cool, frothy saltwater washing up over his bare feet and lapping at his ankles.

He dragged his feet through the surf. Bits of his sailboat had washed up here and there, jagged, broken parts of what represented months of work. Yet he felt oddly calm, almost disconnected. And he realized it wasn't the wreckage of his boat he was looking for as he walked slowly along the shoreline.

It was her.

He was remembering that feeling that had washed over him when he'd held her in his arms. That feeling of peace. His pain had vanished. "God," he whispered. "I wish I could get that feeling back again."

Enya waited her turn in the gilded hall outside the Fay Queen's chambers. She paced nervously back and forth beneath glimmering crystal prisms, and rehearsed again and again what she would say. She'd thought long and hard about this. She'd made her decision, but only Queen Ciarnan had the power to make her wish come true. She'd given it time. Night after night, she'd waited for the yearning in her heart to fade away. But it had only grown stronger. She'd committed an unforgivable sin. She'd fallen in love with a mortal. And she was about to compound the sin with this unprecedented request. But he needed her. She couldn't shake this feeling that something was terribly wrong with Devon, and that he truly needed her.

The doors opened. She heard her name on a voice that tinkled like bells. "Enya. Come forward."

Swallowing hard, Enya stiffened her spine and stepped through the doors. Queen Ciarnan sat upon a throne entirely carved of glittering amethyst. She wore no crown. There was no need. One need only look at her to know she was the Fay Queen.

"You have a request?" Ciarnan asked, and her voice was calm, her blue eyes kind.

"Aye." Enya licked her lips, searching for the lines she'd rehearsed.

"Don't be afraid, child. I already know what it is you wish."

"You do?"

The queen nodded, her red-gold locks moving magically as she did. "You want to be made mortal. To forsake all you are—your magic, your, royal heritage, your home —for the love of a mortal man."

Enya blinked in surprise, but nodded. "Aye. That's what I want. It is the only way I can exist in his world. And I have to be with him. I must"

"And if he doesn't feel the same?"

She felt her eyes widen. "I...I hadn't thought of that"

Ciarnan smiled gently. "I don't believe you've done much thinking at all, child."

"Oh, but I have—"

"You're young. The first gentle breeze of attraction seems to you like the tempest of true love. But only time will prove whether these feelings are true."

"They are true," Enya said, stepping closer and thrusting her chin up in her zeal. "I love him."

"You can't be sure. You're far too young to know love. Would you have me take such drastic action only to learn later that you were wrong? Once you leave the isle and your powers behind, you can never return, you know. And once you give up your wings, the most rare and precious magic you possess, you can never get them back."

"I know. But I love him, Queen Ciarnan. I'm empty without him."

Ciarnan nodded, her eyes filled with understanding. "All the fairies in our realm share similar qualities, Enya. Impulsiveness, boldness, mischievousness, boundless courage. They're bubbling with emotions and passions. But in you, child, those things seem multiplied a thousand-fold. Of patience, however, I fear you have a small supply."

Enya lowered her head, and already tears filled her eyes to brimming.

"Come back to me in a year. If you still feel the same, I'll grant your wish then."

"A year! Gods, Ciarnan, anything might happen in a year. He might be dead, killed by his own recklessness or buried so deep in his despair that I cannot save him. I *can't* wait that long. Something is wrong with him. Terribly wrong. I sense it. I cannot wait—"

"You have no choice. I make this decision for your own good. It's only because I care for you that I—"

But Enya had heard all she cared to hear. She turned and ran from the queen's chambers, and through the great hall and out of the crystal castle. All the way down to the rocky shore she ran, and she flung herself down among the quartz boulders, crying as her heart shattered.

She wasn't sure how long she remained there, half out of her mind with grief. But at some point, a harsh, deep voice interrupted her crying.

"Such a pity, a beautiful fairy child like you, so sad. Such a terrible pity."

Her head came up fast and she dashed the tears from her face with the back of her hand. The troll was short and powerfully built, as all trolls tended to be. His face had that pugnacious quality, with the long, narrow nose's tip pushing down to his upper lip. His hair was wild and blue-black, and his wide-set beady eyes, pale, pale blue.

Enya scrambled to her feet and took a step backward. Trolls were tricksters and powerful magicians. Yet they lacked the power of flight, and were envious of the fairies' wings. They were dangerous. Queen Ciarnan herself often warned her subjects to steer clear of them, should any such being find its way to the enchanted isle. There was never a risk of them finding it again, and leading other dark beings back, since the island was in constant motion. But every once in a while, one might stumble upon it.

"Don't be afraid," he croaked in his deep bullfrog's voice. "I can help you with your problem. And unlike that stubborn despot in the castle, I *will*."

"Don't talk that way about my queen, troll."

The troll smiled, very slightly. "No offense meant. If you're not interested in becoming mortal, then I'll just be on my way. I was only trying to help." He turned, his short legs moving quick as he walked away from her.

Enya bit her lip, gritted her teeth. "Wait."

The troll stopped and stood waiting.

"I...I am...interested. I mean, at least I can hear what you have to say."

"Such a reasonable child," he said, turning to face her once again. "It's quite simple, really. I can make you mortal. I have the power. But I want something in return."

Feeling her heart swell in her chest, Enya whispered, "What?"

"Your wings."

Enya blinked in shock, immediately shaking her head from side to side.

"Oh, silly child, once you become mortal they'll disappear anyway. What harm is there in giving them to me in advance...just in case the spell doesn't work?"

She swung her gaze down to the marble eyes of the troll. "There's a chance it won't work?"

"A small one. Surely this love of yours is worth a small risk?"

Narrowing her eyes, Enya said, "What *kind* of risk?"

"Sit down," said the troll, waving his stubby arm and

broad hand toward a quartz boulder the size of a foot stool. "And I'll explain."

Enya bit her lip, wondering if she should be running away from this prankster as fast as she could. And yet, she sat

"This is the way it works," he said, pacing back and forth in front of her with his hands clasped behind his back. "You give me your wings, and I'll give you a boat that will take you off to the mortal realm. You'll be able to live for three days and three nights there, with no harm to you. In that time, you must make this mortal man fall in love with you. And you must do it without telling him your secret, and without using your magic. If you do either of those things, you will die at once. If he falls in love with you before the three days are up, you will become mortal, and free to live a mortal lifetime with him there."

Enya swallowed hard. "And what if he *doesn't* fall in love with me in three days?"

The troll shrugged. "You'll still be fay. You'll suffer the same effects any pureblood of the royal line would."

"I'll die like a mortal."

He stopped pacing and nodded. "But look at you, Enya. You're as beautiful as Ciarnan herself. Why, any man would have to be insane not to love you instantly."

He was wrong, of course. No one was as beautiful as Queen Ciarnan.

"And you did tell the queen you were willing to give up your magic for this man, didn't you? Surely you wouldn't have done that unless he'd shown some signs of a budding affection for you?"

She lowered her head to hide the blush that crept into her cheeks. It was true, Devon had kissed her with a passion that had set her soul on fire. But he'd been delirious at the time. And probably thought he was dreaming.

"I suppose the only question is, do you believe this love is worth the risk? Will you be content moping about this isle pining away for him for the rest of your days? How will you feel if you lose him, when you had the chance laid at your feet and you turned away from it?"

Enya drew a deep breath, squared her shoulders, and faced the troll. "You're right," she said. "I'll do it. I'll risk anything to be with Devon."

"That's my brave girl."

"What must I do?"

The troll opened his hand, and a sheet of vellum, folded and sealed with wax, appeared in his palm. "Take this. Do not look at it yet. Go to the beach by the light of the full moon, and recite the words on this page. That's all."

She blinked in shock that it was so simple. "But...tonight is the full moon."

"I know," said the troll, and he turned and lumbered away, pausing only once to call back over his shoulder, "Remember, if you use your magic, you've broken the deal, and you will die."

Enya clutched the vellum in her hands and stared at it

until her eyes watered. Finally, she tucked it into the folds of her dress, and turned to walk back home. It would be her last evening with her sister. And she wanted to make the most of it.

She stood on the deserted beach, beneath the light of the full moon. Midnight. The perfect time for magic. She had taken one important precaution. She'd left a note for her sister, telling her everything and imploring her to inform the Queen about the troll, so she could make sure he caused no harm.

With trembling hands she broke the seal and unfolded the vellum sheet. Thoughts of Devon, of that soul-shattering kiss they'd shared, and the pain that haunted his blue, blue eyes, overpowered her fear, and she read the words in a loud, strong voice that was caught up by the wind and carried out to sea.

"Earth, Air, Fire, Sea.

"To Nanraic's terms I do agree,

"I vow by magic, great and small

"For true love, I will venture all!"

The wind sharpened and angled downward, and for a moment she felt it pounding her, yet she stood still, arms uplifted. Odd that it should be so simple. A spell so similar to one a fairy might use herself. But would it work? Was it some kind of trick? The blasting wind slowly died away. And when it was gone, she realized with a startled glance over her shoulders, that her precious wings had gone with it. Her back felt oddly bereft without them. A chill raced up her spine and into her nape, and she saw a small rowboat resting in the sand where none had been before.

Enya drew a deep breath, whispered a prayer, and went to it.

# CHAPTER THREE

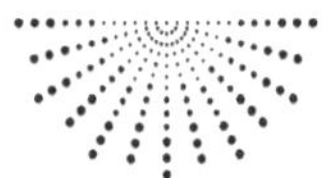

*The Reunion*

Devon sat in the sand, staring out at the gentle, rolling waves and trying to find some peace in his mind. But he couldn't. Night after night, he'd come to the shore to ponder and puzzle over the woman from his dream. He'd never been so moved by a dream before, and he sensed his inability to let go of this one might indicate that it meant something. But for the life of him, he couldn't figure out what.

The full moon held no answers. The sea only whispered more questions. Why would he even *have* a dream like that? He had no interest whatsoever in love or romance. And even if he did, he'd never find a woman like his dream girl. Not anywhere. And even assuming the impossible—that he *was* interested, and *could* find a woman like that one—she wouldn't give him a second glance. The way Devon saw it, that kind of love only came to those who earned it, and he certainly hadn't. He didn't deserve or desire the love and trust of another human being. Not after what he'd done.

Absently scooping a handful of sand and letting it sift through his fingers, Devon stared out at the reflection of the full moon on the gentle swells. And for just a second, he thought he saw something there. A small rowboat, a slender form bending to the oars, a flag of auburn-streaked hair sailing in the wind. He blinked and rubbed his eyes, but when he looked again, the apparition was gone. Vanished.

Damn, it was bad enough he'd dreamed of this fantasy woman. If he started imagining her when he was awake as well, he'd be *really* worried. Nonetheless, he got to his feet, brushed the sand off his jeans, and walked a little closer to the water's edge, squinting and trying to see beyond those ever-growing swells.

Funny, now that he thought about it, the way the waves were picking up in size and strength all the sudden. There was no wind, to speak of, and not a cloud in the sky. Yet each wave rolled farther up the beach, and with more force. If there *had* been any little rowboat out there, it would be a small miracle if its occupant could beach it in one piece. For crying out loud, he could even hear the change in the surf. The waves growled low and deep now, a menacing sound.

Fortunately, there had been no rowboat. Only a flash of Devon's usually docile imagination. He scanned the waves one last time, then failed to dodge a huge, vicious breaker that exploded around his shins, soaking his jeans. Damn. Another followed rapidly, and then another, as Devon high stepped his way back up the beach. Shaking his head in self-deprecation, he turned toward the path that would lead him back up to the house.

"Stupid, worthless bit of wormwood!"

Devon went still at the voice that seemed to come from nowhere. From the darkness, or the sea, or... or his own imagination. It was all but drowned out by those crashing breakers, but he heard it all the same, and even thought he detected a faint Irish accent.

There was a coughing, sputtering sound. "Wretched little troll, giving me a lead-bottomed sieve!"

Devon battled the chill that raced down his spine, told himself it was not the same voice he'd heard singing to him in his dream, and that when he turned he would not see that same beautiful woman. And then he turned around, and he tried to adjust his vision. Her hair was wet. Dripping strag- gles clung to her face. It was dark with sea water and not as curly as he remembered. Most of it was twisted up in a knot in the back, so he couldn't determine its length. Okay, so her resemblance to his dream woman might not be complete. Might not even be all that strong. It had been awfully dark in his dream, after all. He quickly glanced above her shoulders and sighed in relief. She didn't have any wings. Well, then, maybe he hadn't totally lost his mind just yet.

She slogged out of the surf, wringing bunches of the knee-length white dress as she went. She was coming right toward him, though she hadn't seen him yet. "I'll break that long nose of his when I see him again. I'll take his short little arms and tie them up in knots, and then—" Her eyes found his and she stopped her tirade.

Even in the moonlight, he knew they were brown. Deep and dark and as round as any eyes he'd ever seen. He almost fell into them as he stood there, staring at her. And when he finally found his voice, he couldn't think of a thing to say to her. What *could* he say? *Hi. Remember me? We were making out on this very beach the other night, right after you pulled me from the water. Only you had wings then.* She'd probably run screaming for the nearest cop. Or psychiatrist.

He cleared his throat. "Whose arms are you going to tie in knots?"

She blinked, her eyes widening a bit farther. "The horrid little tro- *man* who gave me that rowboat, is who."

"What rowboat?" Devon sent a pointed glance beyond her, but saw only the dark indentations her tiny, bare feet had made in the sand.

"The one that disintegrated before it got me to shore." She came closer to him, dropping the hem of her dress and gathering up another section, twisting it mercilessly in her hands. Water trickled from the cloth and ran down her legs.

She stopped when she stood very close to him. Devon couldn't stop himself from reaching out and picking a bit of green seaweed from her hair. "Are you all right?" he asked her.

She only stared at him and nodded.

He stared back, blown away by the urge that overwhelmed him. The urge to pull her right into his arms and begin again where they'd left off the other night. Only...that had been a dream. Hadn't it?

"Do I know you?" he asked. "You seem so...familiar."

For the first time, her gaze fell away from his. "I only just arrived here in your country this evenin'," she told him.

Devon's shoulders slumped. "Then I couldn't have met you before, could I?"

"I don't suppose so."

He had to touch her. It didn't matter that she was a stranger and had nothing to do with his dream. He had no choice in the matter. His hand clasped hers, in what he hoped seemed like a friendly clasp. "I'm Devon MacKenzie."

She lifted her eyes again, even smiled a little. "I'm called Enya."

No last name? That was interesting, wasn't it?

"Enya," he said softly, and saying her name was almost like kissing her again, the way the soft syllables caressed his tongue as they passed. He shook himself and added, "If you'll tell me where you're staying I'll give you a ride back."

She bit her lower lip. "I'm not sure where I'll be staying, Devon MacKenzie. That rowboat ride was a kind of a spur-o'-the moment decision. I did it before I'd made any other arrangements."

"Impulsive, aren't you?"

Her grin was quick and stunning. "Aye, so I've been told."

"It doesn't matter." He took her shoulders—yes, just an excuse to touch her again—and turned her in the direction of his house. "That's my place, up there," he said, pointing. "Come home with me. We'll get you dried out, and then we'll find you a place to stay. I can take you to wherever you left your luggage, and—"

"Oh, my," she said on a breathy sigh.

He tilted his head. "What is it?"

"Everything I brought with me was in that wretched rowboat."

"Hell," he muttered. "Everything?" She nodded. "Cash?" he asked her. "Credit cards?"

"Everything, Devon." She said it with downcast eyes and a sad shake of her head that seemed a little bit exaggerated. But then she brightened, casting a glance toward the house again. "Oh, but it looks as if you live in a giant of a house. Surely you have room for one soggy female."

He blinked, stunned, only just beginning to hear the warning bells that had been sounding in his head since she'd walked out of the surf. Her story made no sense whatsoever. She was obviously lying, or at least not telling the whole truth. And she hadn't even given him her last name.

"I'm not sure that's such a—"

She faced him, her hands moving to rest lightly on his shoulders, and her eyes boring into his. "Please, Devon. I won't impose for long, I promise. Three days is all I'll be asking' of you. Just three days."

His brows drew together as he studied her face. "What happens in three days?"

"I won't know until they've passed," she told him. "But whatever happens, I won't require your hospitality beyond that."

He shook his head, still baffled. God, was she running from something? Some *one*? Was she a criminal or a witness or a victim or what?

Since her hands had taken the liberty of resting on his shoulders, he didn't think he was stepping out of line when his rose to clasp her tiny waist. "Are you in some kind of trouble, Enya?"

"I very well might be, at that, Devon MacKenzie. And you're the only one who can help me."

Damn. She was trouble with a capital T. And the last thing he wanted to do was to let her waltz into his life for three days and then vanish into the sea as quickly as she'd appeared from it. There was an ominous feeling writhing around in the pit of his stomach, telling him to run for his life.

Then she pressed her small hand to her forehead, and

whispered, "Oh, my," and closed her eyes. Her knees bent, and her body sagged toward his, and the next thing he knew, Devon had a bundle of sopping wet beauty in his arms. And he was left with no choice but to carry her back to the house.

Holding her body against his, despite the circumstances, felt incredible.

# CHAPTER FOUR

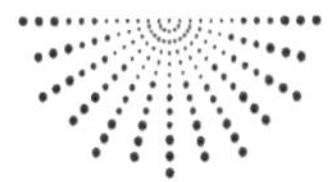

*The Challenge*

Enya had felt a sudden burst of panic when it had seemed Devon would turn her away. So she'd done the first thing that came to her. She'd fainted in his arms. Oh, it wasn't very nice, and certainly wasn't playing fair, but for heaven's sake, her life was on the line, here. She couldn't afford to be subtle.

She opened one eye as he carried her up the porch steps and through the front door, and she saw his proud, strong chin, and his tanned neck. She wanted to trace both with her lips, but of course, it was to soon for that. Oh, goodness, three days! She had three days to make him fall in love with her! She'd thought it would be easy after the way he'd kissed her on the beach. But this time, he hadn't even wanted to bring her home. It might not be as simple as she'd anticipated.

Devon carried her through the house and up the stairs. The place was dark. Belle and George must be sound asleep, it being the wee hours and all. He kicked a door open, and carried her into a room, and a second later he was lowering her onto a bed, and straightening away from her. Oh, bother. She didn't want him away from her. Having his arms around her had been much better.

She moaned a little, and affected a shiver.

"Dammit, you'll catch your death in these wet clothes," he said. And then he was bending over her again, and she felt the warmth of his breath, and the slight tremor in his hands as they moved over the long row of buttons down the front of her dress. He slipped one arm beneath her shoulders, and lifted her off the bed slightly. With his other hand, he pushed the dress down over her right arm. His warm palm skimmed over the bare skin of her shoulder...and stilled there. For the barest instant, he paused with his palm on her skin. He bent his head bent a little, and she heard him inhaling the scent of her hair.

"Damn," he whispered.

He lowered her to the bed and moved away. A second later, a blanket was dropped over her, and then he was gone.

It was Belle who came to her in a short while, undressed her and gently rubbed her down with a warm towel. It was Belle who dressed her in a warm flannel nightgown, took the pins from her hair, brushed it and toweled it dry. It was Belle who didn't ask questions, who just coddled, and who brought hot chocolate, and a down comforter, and who tucked her into bed.

Enya didn't want to sleep. She wanted to be with Devon for every possible moment of her three days. She needed that, if she was going to succeed. But more than likely, Devon was asleep now, too. So she might as well rest, she decided, the better to put her plan into action tomorrow.

Devon sipped scalding coffee, burned his tongue, and swore.

"In a fine temper this morning, aren't you, Devon? I'd never have guessed finding a lost beauty would put you in a bad mood."

He scowled at Belle as she bustled around the kitchen, then shifted his gaze when he heard a muffled chortle from George. George, however, only gave the morning paper a firm shake and remained hidden behind it.

"A stranded woman is the last thing I need around here. Especially one like her."

"One like her?" Belle set a platter of steaming blueberry muffins on the table and propped her hands on her hips. "You mean beautiful? Young? With brown eyes you could drown in and hair like silk, and that lost, needy look about her? Is that it?"

"Hmph." He helped himself to a muffin, split it with his

thumb and pulled it open as blueberry-scented steam escaped its prison. "Dishonest, is what I mean. Wouldn't give more than her first name. Refused to say where she came from. Trouble, Belle. You mark my words, that girl is trouble."

"You could do with an awful lot of that kind of trouble, my boy." Belle sent him a wink and all but skipped into the kitchen.

Devon buttered the muffin and took a bite, sending a sidelong glance through the archway into the living room and the staircase beyond. No sign of her yet. Good. He wasn't sure he could handle seeing her in the daylight...seeing the embodiment of the dream he'd had as he'd lain near death on the beach. Minus the wings, of course. Holding the muffin in one hand, the coffee mug in the other, he pushed his chair back and got up.

George lowered the paper when the chair legs scraped the floor. "Not rushing off, are you, Dev? Wouldn't be polite."

"Polite, hell, I have work to do."

He stalked around the table and through the archway. Escape was within reach. The front door stood just to his left. But she appeared, just like magic, on the stairway at his right.

She paused there, tilting her head slightly and studying him with those unnaturally large brown eyes. He thought he detected a twinkle of gold in them when the morning sun danced over her face. She smiled, and something fluttered in his chest

"Good mornin', Devon."

"Morning." He sent a longing glance toward the door.

"Did I oversleep?"

His gaze snapped back to her again. She wore a long flannel nightgown of snowy white that billowed and floated just above her bare feet. Something Belle had dug out for her, no doubt. And her impossibly long hair, all those burnished curls, surrounded her like a cloak.

"Uh...no. No, not at all," he managed, and then he cleared his throat.

"That's good," she said, smiling again and coming the rest of the way down the stairs. "There's nothing worse than eating breakfast alone. I'm glad I won't have to." She came right up to him, stood directly in front of him, staring up into his eyes. Her smallness made him feel big and awkward. "Unless," she said, glancing at the coffee mug in his hand, "you were leaving."

He looked down at the coffee mug, then back at her. She was doing something to him with those eyes of hers. He could swear she was. "No, I'm not leaving." He nodded toward the dining room, and she turned and preceded him through the archway.

George shot to his feet, his newspaper landing in his oatmeal, and pulled out a chair for her. "Ma'am," he said dipping his head as she sat, just as graceful as an angel.

"You must be George," she told him. "I'm Enya."

"Pleasure's all mine." Before George made it back to his own seat, Belle was calling for him. She stood in the kitchen, holding the door open and smiling like a cat with feathers in its fur. George grumbled, but excused himself and headed into the kitchen.

Leaving Devon alone. With *her*.

Fine. He could deal with this. It had been dark that night on the beach. He'd probably dreamed it all, anyway. And so what if he'd dreamed of a woman who looked like this one? It didn't mean anything. Maybe it had been a premonition or something—not that he'd ever believed in that sort of stuff. Still, he supposed it was possible. Happened to people all the time, he'd heard.

"Did you sleep well?" He asked it just to fill the silence.

"No, actually. I didn't sleep at all well."

He squirmed in his seat. It was not the polite response he'd expected. Nonetheless, that lilting brogue of hers had a way of putting a spell on him. Didn't matter what she said. It was the sound of her voice. Like music.

Like that creature in his dream when she sang to him. Devon shook himself. "Sorry to hear that. Was the room all right? The bed—"

"Oh, the room is fine. Lovely. And that mattress, soft as eiderdown."

Now there was a term you didn't hear every day. Eiderdown. "Then why didn't you sleep?"

She shrugged, reaching for a muffin without taking her eyes from his. That was what was so disconcerting about her, he decided. The way she looked at him. So intensely, and so deeply, and with that soft longing he couldn't identify lingering beneath the sparkle in her eyes.

"I don't know, for sure. Perhaps it was loneliness, keepin' me awake."

Loneliness. A shiver worked right up his spine.

"Why did you leave me to Belle's tender mercies, Devon? Why didn't you stay and tend to me yourself?"

He choked on the muffin, reached for the coffee, and sloshed it over his hand in his haste to bring the cup to his mouth. His eyes watered. But the coffee had cooled and it washed away the muffin blockage. He set the cup down and took a few calming breaths while wiping coffee from his hand with a napkin.

"Now I've gone and shocked you, haven't I?" The mischief in her eyes glittered brighter than a pagan bonfire. When she smiled, her cheeks dimpled.

Devon got to his feet, battling a sensation of something that seemed ridiculously close to fear. "I have to go," he muttered, making no apologies.

"Where?" she asked, and to his horror, she rose as well.

"Nowhere you'd be interested in," he assured her. "Just to my workshop."

"Oh, aye, the big building I saw from my bedroom window."

"Yeah, that's the place." He turned toward escape.

"'Is it there you build your boats, then?"

Frowning, he faced her again. "How did you know..."

"I'd love to see it, Devon," she whispered. "I've always had a passion for the sea."

"P-passion?"

"Aye, the wind whipping my hair, and all that salty

spray soakin' right through my clothes. The sun, kissin' my skin dry, like a lover." She sighed, her eyes dreamy, but still twinkling. "May I come with you, Devon?" That intense gaze bored into his for a long moment. And as if reading his wayward thoughts, she smiled and added, "To the workshop, I mean."

His palms were damp. The nape of his neck, prickling and itching. "I...uh..." He glanced down at her attire, gripping the excuse like a lifesaver. "You're not dressed...and I'm in a hurry."

"Oh, that's all right. I can find my own way." Her bright smile was one of victory. She'd won and she knew it.

"Whatever," he muttered, and hurried out of the room.

It would seem Enya had an ally. Perhaps even two. Belle heartily approved of Enya's plan to walk down to the workshop and ask Devon to give her a tour. And George, though silent on the matter, did smile encouragingly.

Enya's dress of the night before had been cleaned and pressed, and was ready for her to slip on again. She'd brought no others, and she knew now that had been a bit of poor planning on her part. Oh, but she'd been so eager to be with Devon that she'd forgot about being practical.

She did love him so!

And she'd make him love her, too. She would. Enya had never set her mind to something and failed to achieve it. So, she'd be forward, if that was what it took. She'd hound the poor man to madness if need be. But she *would* succeed. Her life depended on it, after all.

She strolled along the well-worn path to the giant of a building, which sat along the top of a slope that rolled gently downward to the sea. It was a long, narrow, one-story structure with the same white clapboard siding and black shutters as the house. Neat as a pin, but lacking the touches that would make it perfect. No flower boxes on the windows, she noted. Nothing green and growing around about it, save the grass, and that needed tending.

The rear of the building faced the sea, and there were stacks of lumber off to one side. A well-worn path led down to the shore, and she saw a dock there, with small sailboats tied up along either side. She continued along the path to the front door, which looked out on a flag-stone walkway that led to a winding, ill-paved road. Above the front door was a hand-tooled sign that read "MacKenzie Brothers Shipyard."

Brothers. Ah, yes. Again, she recalled Devon's younger brother, Bryan, and she wondered where he'd been hiding himself.

But she quickly brushed that thought aside, and without knocking, she opened the door.

Devon crouched at the bow of a small boat, patiently sanding what appeared to be a stubborn rough spot in the wood. Other boats of various sizes, shapes, and stages of construction, littered the building from end to end. And there was a long, narrow table with complex electrical tools laying strewn over it, and big, boxy metal machines scattered about in no order. It looked as if the sky had opened up and rained the contraptions down. Sawdust coated most of the floor.

She closed the door behind her and stepped forward. "She's very beautiful."

He looked up fast, as if she'd startled him. "Thanks," was all he said.

"I've never seen the building of a sailboat before. But I can see you're gifted at it."

"Years of practice," he said, resuming the slow, circular motion of the sandpaper in his hand. "This was my father's business before mine."

"And your brother's," she put in. At his dark glance, she added, "The sign says MacKenzie Brothers."

He only shook his head, which further ruffled his always mussed raven hair, and turned his attention back to his work.

"I've said something wrong, then?"

"No. Look, Enya, I have orders to fill. Work to do. Do you mind?"

She lifted her head with a snap to send her hair flying back away from her face. "Yes, Devon. As a matter of fact, I do." At his astounded expression, she moved closer, slipped around behind him, her hands slipping over his shoulders—oh, and they felt so strong and hard to her touch—and she bent her head down so she spoke close to his ear. "I told you last night, I've only three days to spend here. The least you can do is keep me company."

His body was all stiff. She felt the way he tensed

beneath her hands. He rose slowly to his feet, but didn't turn to face her. "You say that as if I owe you something."

"Now that's an odd thing to say, Devon. 'It's not as if I saved you from a shipwreck, now is it?"

He whirled, his eyes wide and angry. *"What?"*

She gave him what she hoped was an elusive smile. The troll had said she couldn't tell him who she was. But not that she couldn't drop a few hints. "I was merely pointing out, Devon, that it was *you* who rescued *me* when I the sea destroyed my vessel, and not the other way 'round. Indeed, if anyone owes anyone a thing here, surely it is I who owes you."

He blinked, eyes narrowing as he apparently sought hidden meanings beyond her words.

"So, I suppose I ought to leave you be, if that's what you wish. You might well have saved my life. And when someone saves *my* life, I figure the least I can do is show them gratitude. Spend time with them, should they ask it. Or leave them alone, should that be their desire. I'll return to the house now, Devon."

His Adam's apple made a swell in his throat when he swallowed. She knew he was getting her meaning. She'd saved his life and he knew it, or, perhaps, only suspected it. Or maybe he only knew it deep down inside, where you knew the things too strange to be kept on the surface with the mundane. Still, her barb seemed to prick his conscience, just as she had intended.

"It's all right," he said softly, still looking as if he'd just been dealt a blow. "I'll show you around." He reached out to take her arm, but she danced a step away so his grip closed on her hand instead of her elbow. And she twined her fingers with his and squeezed tight.

Devon's eyes fixed on their joined hands, and he stared as if in wonder. And then he returned her squeeze, and led her through the building.

# CHAPTER FIVE

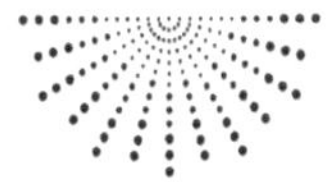

*The Enchantment*

She danced with words, making them spin and leap and do her bidding…and making him think maybe it had been her after all, that night he'd nearly drowned in the shipwreck. Maybe she'd been there, somehow, on the shore, and his mind had only conjured the rest: the wings, and the way she'd seemed to hover above the water as she pulled him to shore.

And the way he'd kissed her.

Damn, had that been real, or a dream? Had *any* of it been real?

He held her hand like a schoolboy with a crush as he led her through the building, showing her the various stages of shipbuilding, and explaining the process. Her hand nestled in his, small and warm, and sending shivers of awareness up his arm and straight to his libido. Especially the way she kept occasionally moving her fingers, just enough to drag a nail across his palm, or rub her forefinger along the side of one of his own, or twist her palm back and forth over his. He'd never dreamed holding bands could be so erotic.

He didn't want this. Even if he *had* kissed her on the beach, he'd been delirious, only semi-conscious. It hadn't meant anything. He didn't want to want her. And he damned well didn't deserve for her to want him.

But she did. And she was doing precious little to hide it

"What beautiful work you do, Devon."

"Thanks."

She used her free hand to stroke a newly varnished bow, her touch light and smooth and arousing to see. He couldn't help but imagine what it would be like to *feel.*

"She looks ready to sail," she observed.

"Yeah, just about. One or two finishing touches and she'll be ready to test on the open water."

She smiled at him, her eyes going wide. "Oh, Devon, let's take her out today! It's been so long since I've been sailing."

Devon's heart sank to his feet "No, Enya."

"But why? It would be such fun. And it's a perfect day, no less."

He swallowed hard, willing her to drop it, but knowing she wouldn't, just by the disappointment he saw in her eyes. "I only sail alone."

Her brows drew together, auburn brows so fine he wanted to smooth his fingertips over them. "Sounds as if it's a rule you've made."

"It is."

"Aye. The question is why?" Her fingers tightened on his, and she turned to look up at him, to scrutinize his face intensely. "I can see in your eyes the subject pains you."

"I don't discuss it," he said, but it didn't carry the none-of-your-damned-business tone he'd intended.

"You can discuss it with me, Devon. I'm not like the others, you know."

"No, I *don't* know. I'm not even sure I want to."

Her eyelids fell suddenly, and he knew he'd hurt her somehow. Odd, since she barely knew him.

"Tell me, Enya, why it is you think I'd be comfortable sharing confidences with someone I've just met, a woman who refuses to tell me her last name, and who won't say where she's come from or why she's here?"

"Ah, sweet Devon, I would if I could," she whispered. And then her chin lowered to her chest.

Devon couldn't help himself. He was compelled to hook a finger beneath that porcelain chin, to lift it until she looked into his eyes again. "Tell me... tell *me something,* Enya."

"Look at me with your heart, Devon, and not just your eyes. Your heart will tell you all you need to know. We're not strangers, you and I."

Damn. The tone of her voice, the look in her eyes...he was damned if he wasn't believing her. She was so familiar, and she had been all along. Even the night of his near-death experience, the night he'd dreamed of her, even then he'd sensed he'd known her before. He'd likened her to the fairy girl of his childhood's fondest dreams.

Narrowing his eyes on her face, he whispered, "Who *are* you, Enya? What is it you want from me?"

"Not so much, Devon. Only your heart"

She said it with a little smile, as if she was making a joke. But Devon believed every word. He caught her other hand in his, so he held them both firmly, in his own. "Don't pin your dreams on my heart, little Enya. My heart died a long time ago. The thing beating in my chest now *is* more like a machine than that tender organ could ever be. There's no more feeling left there. You understand?"

"Aye, Devon. I understand."

"Good."

"If I can't have your heart, then, I'll ask a good deal less. A simple ride in one of your sailboats."

"I told you—"

"You only sail alone, I know. So I'll be forced to borrow one and set out to sea all by my lonesome." She shook her head sadly. "And me, not knowing all I should about sailing. Ah, well, I'll manage, I suppose."

"You can't do that," he told her.

"I can and I will. I've three days in your world, and I intend to savor them."

*In your world. Now what the hell...*

No time to analyze it. She'd whirled around and was heading out the door, and he had to rush after her. She raced around the building, that white dress of hers like a sail in the breeze as she ran down the slope to the water's edge, where several small vessels were docked. Her bare feet made prints in the sand as she dug in, her hair flying wild behind her. Devon ran after her. Tough to get traction in loose sand. She beat him to the dock and leapt onto the wood like a dancer, snatching the lines of the tiny boat on her right and quickly untying them.

"Dammit, Enya, you can't just take one. It's grand theft." He jumped onto the dock just as she jumped off it, and landed in his boat.

Her hands braced on the side, she smiled at him tauntingly. "You should have me tossed into the dungeons, then," she shouted, and quickly turned to work the lines. The sail unfurled; midnight blue, with a brilliant yellow cradle moon. Wind filled it and the boat skimmed the water. Devon ran full tilt to the far end of the dock, and then gave a mighty leap. And he made it, just as the boat cleared the dock.

He lay on his back, where he'd wound up after his ungraceful landing, blinking at a clear blue sky, and surrounded by the sound of her delighted laughter. Sitting up, he gave his head a shake, then sent her a scowl.

"Now, don't be lookin' so angry, Devon. You'd be laughin' too, if you could have seen the picture you made. Flying through the air like a wounded duck, if ever I saw one. Lord a'mercy..." She doubled over, laughing harder, and holding her waist

Devon's lips twitched and pulled at the corners. The

anger he tried to cling to melted like butter at the sound of her laughter, and in a moment, he was smiling fully. "Glad you find my *grace* so amusing," he told her, looking up, meeting her eyes, and freezing there as his smile—and hers—slowly died.

"I love when you smile," she told him. "You don't do it very often, you know."

She was beautiful, this way, the wind and sunlight playing tag in her hair. The light in her eyes. The wonder. And still, that longing.

A gust came up and the boat rocked, reminding him painfully of the last time he'd taken anyone besides himself out onto the fickle sea. He intended to turn back, but she sat down close beside him, covered his hands with her own.

"Just a short sail, Devon, please. We needn't venture far from shore. And I'm a strong swimmer."

"I–"

He broke off, because there was something in her eyes that made it impossible to refuse her. He reached to the floor and snatched up a life vest "All right, a short ride. But put this on."

She held it up, looked it over, wrinkled her nose. "And just how is a woman supposed to entice the man of her dreams wearin' something like this, Devon MacKenzie?"

He swallowed hard. "Just put it on."

She did. But those brown eyes never left his, and when she settled down again, she sat still closer. Her hip touched him, and her thigh and her knee and her shin.

And as he guided the boat into deeper, calmer waters, she lowered her head to rest it on his shoulder, and Devon's heart skipped a beat.

*We're not strangers, you and I.*

No, they were not strangers. Not when he felt this...connected to her, this drawn. The questions remained, but Devon let them fall by the wayside as he maneuvered the boat and manipulated the winds. He relaxed beside her, just a little, and let himself enjoy her nearness. But he went stiff all over again a second later. Because that was when she began to sing.

She sang an entire verse before she saw the look of wonder in his eyes, and when she did, the Gaelic words of the song trailed off into silence.

"You look as if you've seen a ghost," she told him.

"That song..."

"Aye. An old Irish love song, I'm told."

"I've heard it before."

She blinked in surprise, and then bit her lip. Lord, but she'd let herself get carried away in the moment then, hadn't she? She'd let the touch of the wind and the feel of the sea beneath her and the man beside her overwhelm her common sense. Of course he'd heard the song. It was the same one she'd sung to him that night when he'd nearly drowned. She wondered for a moment, if she'd pushed the limits of the troll's rules too far. She closed her eyes, braced herself, and waited. But she didn't die as the seconds passed, and could only breathe a sigh of relief and whisper a prayer of thanks.

"That night...the night of my accident..."

"Oh? You had an accident, you say?" She averted her eyes as his probed and sought.

"You know perfectly well I did. You were there. You...you were singing that same song and then...and then I kissed you." He shook his head hard as if trying to shake water from his hair. "But I thought it was just a dream."

"Perhaps it was, Devon. And perhaps it wasn't. And perhaps you ought to kiss me again, just in case."

Devon looked at her, and she saw his gaze dip to her lips as if against his will before he turned away. He stood abruptly, furled the sail and dropped the anchor, his every movement harsh and quick. He was angry. She couldn't seem to do anything right, she thought miserably. When the boat bobbed in the sapphire waters, he knelt in front of her, gripped her shoulders, bored holes into her eyes with his probing stare. "I have to know what really happened that night."

"And I'll tell you. When my three days are up, 'twill no longer matter, and I'll tell you everything, Devon." She lifted a hand to his face, pushed his hair back, away from his forehead. "Until then, can't you simply enjoy my company as I'm enjoying yours?"

He continued staring, but the anger faded. Something else replaced it in his eyes. His hands on her shoulders kneaded, and his gaze focused once again on her lips. She ran her tongue over them, hoping she saw what she thought she saw in his eyes. Lust wasn't love, but it was a powerful good start. He leaned closer so slowly it was as if he was being pulled involuntarily. His lips hovered a hair's-breadth from hers. And then a nasty little wave slammed into the small boat, rocking it sideways and Devon's hands fell away, his eyes widening in something like panic.

"Damn!" He turned to weigh anchor, and again set the pretty sail flying. And this time, she saw with a heavy heart, they were heading toward shore.

"I'm not ready to go in yet, Devon."

"Then you're a fool."

She winced at his words, but sensed something dark and hurtful lingering beneath them.

"The waves are kicking up," he added in a much gentler tone, sending a glance over his shoulder at her. "You have no idea what can happen out here, how suddenly a pleasure cruise can turn into disaster."

She tilted her head, narrowed her eyes. "But *you* do, don't you, Devon?"

"Yeah. I sure as hell do."

She waited, but he said no more. Just guided the boat back to the waiting dock, secured the lines, and stalked back to his workshop, leaving her alone once more.

# CHAPTER SIX

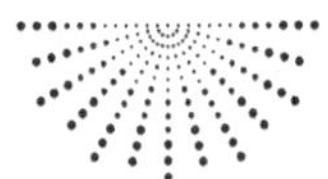

*The Mystery*

He didn't come in for dinner, and Enya was too sick to her stomach to eat. Nearly twenty-four hours now, since her arrival. An entire day with not one hint of progress made. Lord, but she didn't want to die. For the first time, she wondered if she'd made a terrible mistake by bargaining with her magic, her wings. Her very life.

And then she thought about the shivers that had rushed up her spine when he'd kissed her that night on the shore, and the even deeper shudder that had worked through her soul. She must try harder. She had to reach him somehow.

"Odd, that Devon is working so late," George observed

between healthy bites of his pot roast. "It isn't like him to skip meals."

Belle looked worried. Enya sipped her water, which seemed to be the only thing that didn't set her stomach to rebelling, then replaced the glass on the table. "I'm afraid 'tis my fault," she said softly. "I made him take me sailing this morning, and—"

"He took you out in one of the boats?" Belle's graying eyebrows rose high, puckering the skin of her forehead.

"I didn't give him much choice in the matter, I'm afraid."

"I see," she said, sending a knowing look to her husband. "Well."

"Good for you," George said. "About time he got over this nonsense. Isn't good for a man to isolate himself the way he has since—"

"George!"

George looked up, bit his lip. "No man is an island, sweetheart. That's all I'm saying."

Enya sat a little straighter, thinking she might have stumbled onto something, here. Something that would help her understand Devon better, a clue as to what haunted his blue eyes. "Then," she said carefully, not wishing to appear nosy. "Devon is of a mind to live his life all alone?"

George nodded, his lips forming a thin, disapproving line.

"But why?"

"Punishing himself, is my guess. But then, I'm no head shrinker."

Belle patted Enya's hand with her own. "It's not our place to tell you Devon's secrets, dear. Besides, it would do more harm than good if he found we had." She gnawed her lower lip, seeking her husband's gaze as if in search of approval. He nodded almost imperceptibly. And Belle nodded back before she went on. "Still, Enya, if you could get *him* to tell you—"

"Get me to tell her what?"

Devon's deep voice came from the archway, and all three of them jumped like children caught doing something they oughtn't. Belle and George quickly returned their attention to their meals, but Enya held Devon's inquisitive stare, lifting her chin, determined not to be less than honest with him. There wasn't time for lies.

"I was askin' Belle what haunts those sea-blue eyes of yours, Devon, and what makes you act such an ogre to me. But she wouldn't tell me."

"Wise of her." He came the rest of the way into the room, yanked out a chair and sat down. He reached for the bowl of baby vegetables all mingled together and swimming in broth, and ladled some into his dish.

"I agree. It will be far more meaningful when you tell me yourself. So, Devon, why *are* you such an ogre to me?"

His eyes narrowed as he looked up at her, ladle still in his grip. "This is me, Enya. You don't like it, you can always leave a couple of days early."

Enya held his gaze, and she could feel the energy

zapping between her eyes and his. Anger, yes, there was that. He was certainly less than pleased at her prying. But there was more, too. A pull. A magnet that nearly drew her right out of her chair and into his arms. And he felt it, too. He *must.*

"I'll not leave you, Devon. Not until the fates force it."

"Funny, I could have sworn you told me you were leaving in two more days."

"Same thing," she whispered, and she lowered her eyes to the dish of food as her stomach twisted.

"The sooner the better, as far as I'm concerned."

"Devon, really!" Belle threw her napkin on the table as she rose to her feet.

"No. It's all right," Enya told her. Though her suddenly tight throat made the words come soft and coarse. Belle shook her head slowly, but sat back down. Enya rose, though, pushing away from the table. "I believe I'll go on up to my room now, if you'll all excuse me." No one said a word. They just watched her as she turned and moved through the dining room. But something stopped her, something made her turn and step up to Devon's chair, despite that his spine went rigid at her approach. He didn't turn, so she leaned over him, until her lips were very close to his ear, and she whispered, "You need me as much as I need you, Devon MacKenzie. I only hope you realize it, before it's too late." She brushed a gentle kiss across his cheek, and then she turned and hurried away.

～

Belle and George glared at him after Enya's footsteps died away. They couldn't have heard what she'd whispered to him. He had, though, dammit. He still heard it. Her heartfelt whisper breezed through his mind over and over, making him grit his teeth and order it silent.

He met their accusing stares. "You don't know what she did today," he told them. "Listen, she deserved it. Dammit she took a brand-new boat after I told her not to, and left me with no choice but to..." Sighing, he shook his head. "Never mind. Why the hell am I explaining myself, anyway? I'm a grown man."

"You're a grown fool," George said. "Any blind man could see that girl's falling for you."

"Yeah, well I don't want her falling for me. I don't want anyone falling for me."

Belle shoved her plate away. "Maybe it's time you did! And even if you're too stubborn to admit that, there was no call for you to go and make her cry."

His eyes widened at the final phrase. The thought of Enya crying made, his stomach turn over. "I didn't—she wasn't—" He glanced over at George, not sure trusting Belle's version of things was a good idea at the moment. "Was she?"

"What crying? Oh, yes indeed, Devon. Tryin' hard to hold them back, you know, but those big tears managed to slide right down her cheeks before she turned to go."

"Hope you're proud of yourself," Belle snapped, getting up and heading into the kitchen with her hands full of dishes, apparently not realizing—or more likely, not giving a damn—that Devon had yet to eat.

George turned his attention back to his food, cutting Devon's presence off like snapping off a light switch. He couldn't believe these two who'd practically raised him were siding with a girl they'd only known for a day.

And he couldn't believe he'd made her cry. It wasn't her he was angry with. It was himself. Because he wanted her more with every breath he drew, and he knew it wasn't just physical. He didn't want this. She was making him feel things he'd decided he would never feel, things he didn't deserve to feel. But it would pass, because he sensed she'd been honest when she'd told him she had only three days. He knew, instinctively, that she wouldn't stay longer. He thought she might want to, and at the same time, he was almost certain she'd stay longer if he asked her to. But he wouldn't ask. He'd wait it out, stick to his guns, protect himself from the lure of her, until her time was up. And then it would be over, and things could go back to normal.

No beautiful face across the table in the morning. No curious questions and childlike enthusiasm. No one pestering him in the shop. No one making his heart beat for what felt like the first time in two-years. There would be no one, once she left. No one at all.

"I'm going for a walk," he said, and to his own ears his voice sounded lifeless. He got up and left without having touched a bite of his food

He walked and walked and walked. He found himself in town a few hours later, and stopped in at a diner for a burger and fries. All the nutritional value of cardboard, he thought as he consumed the salt and grease. He took his time, because he was in no hurry to get back to her, to see her again and try to deny what he was feeling in every cell of his body. He ate slowly, and then ordered more fries, and nibbled on them, and then ordered a slice of cherry pie. He managed to make that slice of pie last through three cups of coffee. But it did no good to stay away from her, because he was thinking of her anyway–or of someone very like her.

Those dreams he'd had as a child.... God, it was uncanny how vividly he recalled them. She would come, that fairy child. She'd take his hand, and twinkle her big brown eyes at him, and dare him to come with her, and he'd always accept. Together they'd explored rain forests, watching lions or elephants from amid the greenery. They'd explored castle ruins, and rolled down lush green hillsides.

She'd been so important to him. She'd been an imaginary friend, yes, but she'd also been his best friend. And he was damned if he could shake the feeling that she'd come back to him now, all grown up and more beautiful than ever.

He ordered another piece of pie, and started on a second carafe of coffee.

It was after ten p.m. when he finally left the diner, and by the time he'd walked the eight miles back home it was pushing midnight. And he was safe.

Or...he thought he was safe.

He went up the front steps, reached for the front door...and the wind picked up, just enough to carry her voice right to his ears. She was singing again, a different song, this time. Something plaintive and unspeakably sad. It was coming from the beach.

It might as well have been a siren's, because it worked the same way. It lured him, called to him, tempted him, until he turned away from the house and stared down toward the white sand dunes standing at the lip of the blue-black sea. And she was there. Her white dress billowing like an angel's robes, her ankles surrounded by froth and foam. She walked along the shoreline slowly, her steps keeping time with the song, and she tipped her head back and sang as if her heart was breaking.

And maybe it was.

*Stupid thought. Why would it be? She barely knows me.*

Wrong. She knew him. Maybe too well.

Her song tugged, and he went like a man sleepwalking, knowing he was going, but somehow unable to stop himself. One foot dropped in front of the other, and he felt as if he was just an observer, watching some poor fool sailor stupid enough to submit to the lure of the sirens' song.

# CHAPTER SEVEN

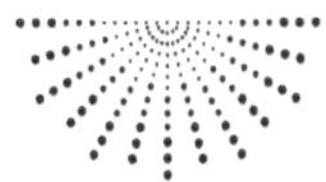

*The Revelation*

She felt him before she saw him. Fay sense. It wasn't magic, really. Just a part of who she was. She wondered whether she would lose it, if she won this battle, passed this test, and became a mortal woman. And then she decided she might never know, because so far, she was failing.

And for some reason, that bit of knowledge wasn't the most important thing on her mind. The thing that was, was Devon's pain. She could see it, so very clearly. It shone from his eyes and cried from his soul. It was in his walk, his voice, his very essence. A hurt that enveloped him like a shroud, refusing to let him feel pleasure or happiness or love ever again. And suddenly, her own life and death didn't seem nearly as important as removing that funereal shroud from Devon's vibrant soul.

Her song died away, or was carried off by the sea breeze. Devon stood close behind her, not saying anything, just standing there. She turned, looked at him, but he was staring past her, out to the rolling whitecaps and foamy waves. Lord, but his eyes were haunted.

"Ah, Devon," she whispered, and her hand cupped his face, ringers slipping into his hair. "Don't you know I'm here for you? Can't you see me here?"

"I see you. I can't stop seeing you."

"I've come to make it better, Devon."

He blinked the moisture from his eyes, but continued staring at the sea.

"I didn't realize it at first, of course," she went on, rubbing a lock of his hair between thumb and forefinger as the wind whipped the rest. Like satin, his dark hair. Black satin. "I thought I'd come for selfish reasons. But perhaps I was wrong. Because there's no such thing as coincidence. It was not by chance I chose that night to visit you. It was not longin' alone that told me I must come to you now. You need me, Devon. You wished for me. That's why I'm here."

He dragged his gaze from the sea, and finally locked it with hers. "There's nothing you can do."

"Aye, so you believe. But you must let me try. Otherwise, your wish will be wasted."

He stared at her for a long moment, unblinking, searching.

"You've nothing to lose, have you, Devon? And if telling me about what troubles you does you no good, well, you've lost nothing. I'll be gone soon, and you can pretend you remained stoic and solitary straight to the end. You can pretend I was never here, make believe I was a dream, the way you've done before."

He blinked at her in astonishment, but Enya only smiled. She took his hands in hers, and pulled him with her to a dry patch of sand where the tide didn't quite reach. "Sit," she told him. "Talk to me. You know you want to."

He sat. She did, too. She pulled her dress over her knees and hugged them close, and waited for him to begin. And when he didn't, she said, "Your brother Bryan used to live here, with you. He was your partner and your friend."

"I loved him."

Enya nearly sighed in relief. He was talking, at least "How did you lose him, Devon? Was it to the sea?"

Devon nodded. "But it wasn't just him. He had a wife, Sarah. Young and shy and beautiful... and expecting their first child."

Sadness poured over her soul, making her heart feel heavy all of the sudden.

"She wanted to sail down the coast. I was against it, but Bryan never could say no to her. I insisted on going with them. I knew...something inside me knew they shouldn't go. Why the hell didn't I listen to it?"

"Most men wouldn't even have heard it, Devon. You tried."

"Not hard enough. We ran into weather fifty miles south. Sails ripped to shreds, that little boat foundering like a guppy, fighting twenty-five-foot swells. Radio bringing nothing but static. I put out an S.O.S., but damned if I knew whether anyone received it. And about that time the mast came down. Sarah never even knew what hit her."

Enya bit her lip. "She.... she died?"

"Before she hit the deck," he said.

"And your brother?"

"He lost it. He just lost it. Fell down on top of her, there on the deck screaming, shaking her, begging her to wake up.... God, it was a sound I'll never forget. It haunts my dreams."

She closed her eyes and closed both of her hands around one of his, squeezing gently.

"When he realized he couldn't bring her back, he...I don't know, he went wild. Picked her up in his arms. Knocked me on my ass when I tried to stop him. And then he just...he just went over the side. Sank out of sight. I went in after him, but it was as if the sea had swallowed them both. I couldn't find him. I was still diving and searching when the Coast Guard arrived. They pulled me out of the water, tranquilized me. Hell, if they hadn't, I'd probably still be out there." He shook his head slowly.

"Perhaps you're thinking you ought to be," she whispered.

He blew a sigh. "Why not? Why should I be here, safe and sound, while my brother and his wife and their baby..." The hand she held curled into a fist before he pulled it free. "Fate got it backwards, Enya. It should've been me hit by that mast, not her."

"That's simply not true, Devon."

His head jerked toward her. "How can you say that? How can it not be true? They had so much to live for, the two of them. A baby on the way, a new marriage. They were so in love."

"Aye," she whispered. "I imagine they were. But every soul knows when it's time to move on."

His brows drew together.

"You've no way of knowing what lay ahead for them. You imagine they would have had long lives filled with unending bliss. But what if that wasn't what fate had in store, Devon? Suppose only heartache and pain awaited them, instead of this bliss you've imagined? Suppose one was bound to leave the others, or two were bound to leave the one, alone and grieving? Suppose on some level—not a conscious one, mind you—they simply decided to move on together, rather than to remain and be separated?"

Devon gave his head a shake, then searched her face. "What kind of a notion is that?"

"The only kind that makes sense. Souls move on when they're ready. Rarely before."

"How can you know that?"

She shrugged. "How can you not?"

He stared hard at her for a long moment, then shoved

himself to his feet and began pacing toward the water. She rose as well, keeping pace.

He walked rapidly, right to the water's edge, and stared out at the dark horizon as waves lapped over his feet. And finally, he shook his head hard. "No. No, I don't believe it. It wasn't part of some grand scheme, there was no meaning, no reason. It just happened."

"And because it happened to them instead of you, you feel you've no right to a life. Since their happiness ended, you won't allow yourself to feel any. Instead you go about in your beautiful boats on nights when the worst sorts of storms murmur their dire warnings in your ears. You shake your fists at the black night sky, and you challenge it. And part of you wishes the darkness would win. It nearly did the last time, Devon."

"It wasn't like that"

"No? How was it, then?" Her hands curled over his shoulders, felt the tension there.

"Not suicidal," he told her. "That kind of thing isn't in me, Enya. I was angry when I went out that night. Furious. Raging, just as I've been since they died. Going out in that storm...I was lashing out at the sea and the sky and maybe even God Himself, I guess. Daring Him, yeah, but I never had any doubt I'd survive. Beat Fate. Petty vengeance, at best. At worst, I suppose you could call it a temper tantrum."

"But it wasn't the first time you've taken such a risk."

He bent low, scooped up a small, perfectly formed shell

and pitched it into the waves. "Probably won't be the last, either."

"Suicidal or not, Devon, you could be killed. Last time–"

"Last time I probably would have drowned, if not for you." He turned slowly and stared into her eyes. "I don't know how, but I know you were there. You were, weren't you?"

She averted her eyes. "I..."

"Don't lie to me. If I need anything from you right now, Enya, it's the truth."

"What you need from me is healing." *And magic,* she thought. Her magic could help him see the truth. But she wasn't allowed to use it here. Only...maybe she could let *him* use it.

"Nothing can give me that. Healing. It's never gonna happen."

Enya bit her lip. "I used to feel the same way," she whispered. "When my mother left my sister and me, it seemed I would never be happy again. But she left me something." Slipping one hand into the vee of her neckline, she closed it around the tiny black conch shell, with the bright pink inside. She thought it over, and made her decision, nodding once, firmly when she did. If she were to die here two short days from now, she'd have no more need of the shell. And if she were to live, it would mean her every wish had come true. And she wouldn't need it then, either.

She couldn't use her magic to help Devon. But she could give the shell and the magic it possessed to him, and let him help himself. She took the cord from around her neck and cupped the shell in her hands.

He only frowned at her.

Bending down until her dress pooled in the froth that surrounded her feet, she dipped the shell into it, filling it with water. And then she straightened again, turning 'round until the moonlight from above flashed on the water in the shell, turning it to liquid silver that winked and shone.

"Hold out your hands, Devon."

"What?"

"Just do it, just like this."

Slowly, Devon's hands rose, palms cupped to receive the shell, and closing her eyes, Enya placed her shell there. Not a drop of silvery water spilled. A good sign, she thought.

"The magic of this shell works only for its owner. Therefore, I give it to you."

He frowned at her solemn tone, glancing down at the shell, and then up at her again. "I don't know what you're—"

"Open your heart, Devon," she whispered. "Look. See the truth that eludes you, and put an end to this torment."

He frowned hard, his narrowed eyes studying her face, as he stepped closer to her, then, almost hesitantly, dipping lower to focus on the shell, and the suddenly gleaming water it held.

"The shell is a doorway. It only opens when the need is

strong, as I believe your need is tonight," she explained. "It will show you what you need to see."

He looked down at the glistening water as it took on a brilliant white gleam, so bright the light touched his face and sparkled in his eyes. Suddenly his frown vanished. His eyes widened and his jaw fell. *"Bryan..."*

Enya looked down at the apparition, the face of Devon's brother floating in the shell where the water had been, emitting that white light.

"Bryan," Devon said again. Enya touched his face with her palm. And then she turned and moved silently away, leaving him to see what he needed to see, praying it would be enough to save him from the darkness of his soul.

Devon had no idea what was happening, much less *how* it was happening. But there, in that shell that had suddenly become a miniature television screen—or, a tiny doorway of some kind—he saw a scene unfold before his eyes. He saw his brother, Bryan, looking happier than Devon had ever seen him, running through a lush green, wildflower-dotted meadow beneath a white-hot sun, with a giggling little girl on his shoulders. Devon blinked, but the vision remained. At the edge of the meadow, Sarah sat in the deep grasses with her legs curled beneath her, watching her husband and child romp. There was a look of utter peace on her pretty face. There were wildflowers in her hair.

And even as Devon gaped and shook himself and tried to make sense of this, his brother stopped playing and turned. And it was as if he was looking straight into Devon's eyes.

*You don't have to understand it all, Dev,* Bryan said, though his lips didn't move. And Devon didn't actually *hear* his voice. It sort of floated into his mind. *Just know that I'm where I need to be right now. We all are. And none of it was your fault. We're okay, Devon, but we can't be completely at peace until you get past this. Get rid of the guilt. Find your own happiness, brother.*

"I can't. Dammit, Bryan. I should have been able to find you, to pull you out... I should—"

*Love us, Devon. Think of us with love, not guilt.*

"I do! I do love you!"

*I know.* The apparition smiled, the crooked grin that was so familiar it made Devon's heart twist. *I've always known.*

The vision in the shell rippled and faded, and became crystalline water once more. Devon stared at it, tears clouding his eyes. "Wait, don't go!" He shook the thing, but that only resulted in the water it held slopping over his hands. "Bryan..."

Devon began to tremble. He let the shell fall at his feet, and he hugged himself as unearthly chills raced through him, and he lifted his head to search the night sky as if the answers might be found there. "Bryan!" he yelled, and it was a cry of anguish.

A cry that died away as three shooting stars cut a

glowing arc through the night, one after another, all following the same path.

Devon sank into the cool, damp sand, the shock and the wonder of it all making his knees too weak to hold him. And slowly, he drew his gaze away from the sky and looked toward the house just in time to see Enya as she fluidly mounted the steps, crossed the porch, and stepped inside.

How had she done this...this magic?

He remembered the way she'd appeared to him the night of his accident, the way she'd appeared to him in his childhood dreams. The wings. And he remembered the word that had flitted into his mind the first time he'd seen her, the word she herself had used that night as he lay half-conscious, clinging to her. *Fairy.*

# CHAPTER EIGHT

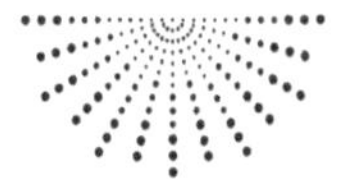

*The Dawning*

Cool water washed over his fingertips, and Devon opened his eyes. He saw the sea, its foamy waves rolling ever closer to where he lay, coated in sand. The fiery orange upper curve of the sun rested on the horizon, big as the world, ascending slowly to take possession of the sky.

He'd fallen asleep on the beach. And the rest had been a dream. A dream, that's all it had been. A strange, vivid, ludicrous dream. He hadn't spoken to Enya out here last night. And she hadn't given him any magical seashell, and he hadn't talked with his dead brother.

He'd eaten too much junk food, and he'd done too

much vigorous walking in the hot sun, and he'd slept on the beach and he'd dreamed. Period.

He sat up and scrubbed the sand from his hair with both hands. And then he stopped. Because lying beside him in the white sand was a pure black conch shell, small enough to fit in the palm of his hand. It was bright pink inside, and there was a tiny hole bored through one end, where someone had strung a cord. A now familiar chill raced up his spine, but his mind refused to believe....

No, Enya must have been walking on the beach and lost this thing. That was all. He snatched it up and ran toward the house with it, determined to return it to her, and prove to himself that nothing had happened.

The screen door banged shut behind him, and Belle looked up from her dusting to smile at him. "My, but it was a beautiful night last night, wasn't it, Devon? Enya said you'd decided to sleep on the beach. Did you see that wonderful display?"

He halted in his tracks, halfway to the stairs. "What display?" he asked without turning.

"Why the shooting stars, of course! Three of them, right in a row. I've never seen the like. Come, Devon, you couldn't have been out there and not seen it."

He blinked, pressed his lips tightly together, swallowed hard. *It was real*

*Bullshit.*

"Where is Enya?"

"Oh, that one! Insisted on making breakfast, the imp, though I daresay she doesn't know her way around a kitchen any too well. Still, she was so eager, I couldn't say no to her."

That made sense. He'd been having a hell of a time saying no to her, himself. He changed direction, heading through the archway into the dining groom, and through the door at the far end that led to the kitchen.

And then the questions, the confusion, the mystery—all of it—just faded away and Devon MacKenzie laughed.

Enya stood at the counter with her back to him, elbow-deep in gooey dough. Her arms and hair sported sprinkles of flour and smudges of shortening. To her left, the gas range's front burner blasted full force beneath a smoking skillet full of charred sausage links. To her right, the coffee maker churned in protest as streams of thick-looking brew coursed down its sides.

He saw her back stiffen and tried to stifle his laughter. He was almost successful, in fact, but then she turned to glare at him, and she pulled her hands from the dough that didn't seem quite willing to relinquish its sticky grip. He held on, right up until she lifted a hand to push her hair out of her eyes, and smeared a glob of the stuff across her forehead. But that was his undoing. He nearly doubled over as the laughter burst from somewhere deep in his gut. He crossed his arms around his belly, fought for breath, and laughed all the harder.

"Of all the rude and ill mannered hosts I've ever heard tell, Devon MacKenzie, you take the cake." She tried to wipe the dough from one hand with the other, but since both were well coated, the effect was minimal.

"I'm sorry. If you could *see* yourself..." And that was all he managed, because he got lost in laughter once more.

It only died when he realized they were no longer alone in the kitchen. Belle had stepped in from the dining room, and stood stock still in the doorway, staring at him, wide-eyed. For some reason her lower lip was trembling. George, too, seemed to wonder at the commotion. He came in through the back door, and then stopped, still holding it open and blinking at Devon as if he'd suddenly sprouted a second head.

"Saints be praised," Belle whispered. She folded her hands to her breast, closed her eyes. "He's laughing."

She looked across the room at George, and both of them turned toward Devon, with canary-eating grins on their faces. Belle was blinking back tears.

Devon choked back another round of mirth, cleared his throat "Of course I'm laughing. *Look at her.*"

Belle did just that, only instead of laughing at Enya's gooey hands and flour-splattered face, she beamed. And then she shook her head, dabbed at her eyes with the hem of her apron, and crossed the room to grab George's elbow and lead him back outside. As they left, Devon noticed, Belle leaned her head on George's shoulder.

Enya had moved over to the sink and was trying to turn the knobs with an elbow, while keeping her dough-encased hands up like a freshly scrubbed surgeon. He almost lost it again, but bit his lip and moved up beside her, turning off the burner as he passed. He reached past her to crank the faucets, adjusted the water to a tolerable warmth, and then leaned against the sink while she washed the dough from her hands and forearms.

"So," Enya said, squirting a bit of dish detergent into her palm for good measure. "You think this is funny, do you?"

"Hilarious." His lips were still quirking at the corners as he watched her. And it was quite by accident and totally unintentional when he reached up to brush a bit of flour from her cheekbone with his thumb. And then his smile died, and he thought that even in bread dough, she was the prettiest thing he'd ever seen.

"I suppose it serves me right," she said in her magical Irish brogue. "Trying to impress you with my domestic skills was not the best idea I've had of late."

He blinked, surprised yet again by her blunt honesty. So she'd been trying to impress him.

"Cooking is not something I've had much call to do."

"Apparently not," he said, and he glanced at the box from which she'd taken the sausage links-and chuckled all over again. "Those sausages are supposed to be nuked, not fried."

She frowned at him, and he nodded in the direction of the microwave. But she only tilted her head, still looking puzzled.

"It's a microwave, Enya. Haven't you ever seen one before?"

"No," she admitted, and sent him a worried glance. "Does that make me frightfully ignorant in your eyes, Devon?" When he only stared at her, his mind refilling itself with all those questions he'd forgot about, she turned off the water and wiped her hands on a towel, lowering her head. "I guess it must."

He took the towel from her, lifted it to her face. "If I wanted a woman who could cook, I'd work on stealing Belle away from George."

"Oh, that you could never do. Those two are deep in love." She closed her eyes and let him clean her face. But all of a sudden he was more interested in kissing it. He clenched his jaw and finished the job, dabbing the sprinkles and spatters from her neck, running his ringers over her smooth skin as he did.

"Tell me, Devon," she whispered as he traced the curve of her neck again and again. "How long has it been since you've laughed aloud like that?"

His hands stilled, fingertips poised over the fluttering pulse point. He hadn't thought of it before. But of course, that was it. That was why Belle and George had seemed so blown away. "I can't say for sure," he told her. "But it's been a while."

"Since your brother and sister-in-law died, I suppose."

He closed his eyes. Here it was, the confirmation he'd been both anticipating and dreading. "So it really happened. I really did tell you about that trip."

"Aye, Devon, that you did."

He pulled the shell from his shirt pocket letting it dangle from its cord. "And this?"

She took it from him, and gently lowered it over his

head. "I gave this shell to you last night. And I hope you'll keep it always."

He swallowed the sudden lump in his throat and fingered the shell that hung around his neck. "I saw my brother in this shell. I know that's not possible, but—"

"Everything's possible, Devon."

He studied her intently. "Who are you really, Enya?"

She averted her big brown eyes, and he knew just by looking at them that she wasn't going to tell him. "Who do you think I am?"

"I'm not sure. I think...I think you're not...like other people. I think you're maybe...not even... mortal."

"Oh, I'm mortal, Devon. A bit too much so."

"You're magic."

"Everyone is magic, deep down inside. They only need to realize it to make it so."

"You're not of this world, are you? You're composed of....of something else. Some mystical stuff not found in the rest of us."

"I promised you once that I'd tell you the whole truth before I left here. But I can't tell you just yet, Devon. You must be patient."

She started to turn away from him, but he caught her shoulders, held her eyes. "Tell me this much. What I saw last night in the depths of this shell...was it some trick, some kind of spell you cast or whatever it is you do? Or was it...was it real?"

"Oh, it was real, Devon. As real as your hands on my shoulders right now, and the way they make me feel. As real as your breath on my face, and your lips so close I can almost taste them. That's how real it was. Your brother is fine. His family is happy and whole. You're the one in agony, love, not them."

He stared down into her eyes, and he saw that sparkle, that twinkle that had never lived in the eyes of a human being. And he whispered, "I've known you all my life, haven't I?"

She nodded.

"You used to come to me...somehow...in my dreams. We played together. We—"

"We explored ruined castles and mysterious caves and virgin forests. Aye, Devon, it was a special time. But you grew up. You stopped believing in your fantasies, and I couldn't visit you in your dreams any more. But I couldn't stay away, either."

"Why?"

"Oh, surely you don't need to ask me that! I've crossed worlds to come to you here, but I cannot stay. I cannot stay unless you get past your useless regrets and open your eyes." She threw the dishtowel down, turned, and left the kitchen. He heard her go upstairs to her room, heard the door slam. He gave his head a shake to clear it, but of course, it didn't work. She was real. She was here, the object of his childhood fantasies. And she needed something from him, something too scary for him to think about.

Work, he needed to work. And maybe, eventually, all

of this would make some kind of sense. He headed out to the shop, leaving Enya to the house for a while.

83

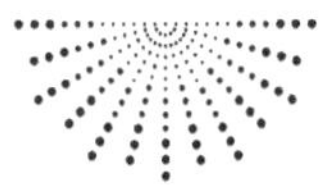

# CHAPTER NINE

*The Flame*

He threw himself into his work, though all day he was distracted, constantly glancing toward the shop door, half expecting her to come through it and insist he take her sailing, or begin another round of questions.

And when he wasn't doing that, he was wondering about her, wondering whether she was real or a figment of his imagination, wondering whether he'd dreamed the past two days and would wake up to find they'd never happened. And though that theory was the one which made the most sense, he found it to be the one hardest to believe. Enya was real, as real as he was. And she was there, for a little over one more day, she was in his life. So what was he doing out in the shop?

Well, that was a stupid question. He was out there because he didn't want to get involved in a relationship with a woman.

*Why?*

Because he couldn't. He couldn't go about his life as if nothing had happened. Dammit, his brother was dead. *His* life was over. How could Devon pretend that didn't matter? How could he?

*But Bryan's okay. You know that now.*

Yeah. He knew that now, as little sense as it made. He'd never thought much about life after death, but there seemed no other explanation for the vision he'd seen in the conch shell...or those three shooting stars. No matter how much his practical mind rebelled at the idea, in his heart, he knew his brother was okay. And as he let that knowledge settle in, he realized he hadn't been feeling the same way since last night. His bitterness, his anger...they'd faded. In their place was some kind of peace. Some kind of knowing that left him...better.

Enya had given him that

He was left with no further excuse for avoiding her. He was left wondering what man in his right mind would deliberately keep his distance from a woman like her. But of course, he knew the answer to that too. A frightened man, that was what kind. And he was, he admitted a little reluctantly, afraid of her. The feelings she aroused in him were too intense not to be frightening. And beyond all that was the mystery of her. Who she was, where she'd come from, how she could do the things she did. And why in hell she'd never heard of a microwave oven, for God's sake.

*She said she'd tell you. She said to be patient and she'd explain everything.*

True enough. And who was he that he couldn't wait another—he glanced at his watch; nine p.m.—another twenty-seven hours for his answers?

He'd been a fool. A coward. And when he really let himself explore his reasons for that, he found one more. Probably the biggest one of all. He'd lost his brother, and it had hurt beyond measure. He didn't want to let himself feel anything at all for Enya because she might leave in the end. He might lose her, no matter what he did. He'd been guarding his feelings like a greedy dog with a bone. But despite his best efforts, the imp had carved a place for herself in his heart

He wanted her. He knew she wanted him. He had to ask himself which would be worse. To relish the little time he had left with her and then be forced to let her go? Or to let her go, and never have taken the chance. Never even to have known what it might have been like to hold her, to kiss her, to....

The soft creak of the shop door alerted him. But he'd have known she'd come in even if it hadn't. There was a lightness to the air when she was near. A warmth that permeated every molecule she touched. She glowed somehow.

He rose from his squatting position beside the bow he'd been sanding, dropped the sandpaper, and turned to look at her. Her white dress stood out in the dimness of the shop, making him think of angels.

"I'm sorry to bother you, Devon. Belle asked me to check on you. You missed dinner again, and she's worried." She glanced down at her dress and then back up at him again. "Why are you looking at me that way?"

He shook his head in self-deprecation. "Enya, would you like to come sailing with me?"

Her brows rose in perfect arches above wide, round eyes. "Do you really need to ask?"

He smiled, and it wasn't forced. Fully natural, completely without effort. "Good. Come on." He moved forward, took her small hand in his much larger one, and stared down at the picture that made. Her hand nestled in his. Something yawned and stretched inside him. Some part of himself that had been asleep for far too long was coming awake now. Fully awake.

He held her hand that way as he led her through the shop, and out the back door, the one that faced the beach. And she didn't say a word as they walked through the sand, or as he untied a small vessel and helped her aboard. She sat, waiting, watching him with those deep brown eyes, and she seemed expectant and wary and half afraid.

As Devon unfurled the sail and the boat began skimming the waves, further and further from shore, she seemed to relax a bit. Enough to question him, he discovered, when she softly asked, "Why now, Devon?"

He angled the boat in a southward direction and let the wind push them along. And then he relaxed, one hand on the rudder. "I don't know if I can tell you why," he said slowly, giving it a great deal of thought. "Maybe because I've realized it's time I said good-bye to Bryan. And this is where I have come to do that. Or maybe it's just that it's been too damn long since I've actually enjoyed sailing."

He turned his face to the wind, because he hadn't realized how true those words were until he'd spoken them. He hadn't enjoyed this, not since Bryan's death. But now, the sea's breath in his face and the spray dampening his clothes, and the moonlight glittering on the water reached deep inside him. All those old feelings returned. His love of the sea, of sailing, of becoming one with the waves and the boat. Those things were still there, alive and well. He'd foolishly believed them dead.

"But you're enjoying it now?"

Her voice came to him softly, like part of the breeze in his ears, and he nodded. "Yes."

"You could have done so without me along, Devon."

"Maybe. But you're enjoying it, too, aren't you?"

"That I am."

Something in her tone made him turn to look at her. She stood with her hands braced on the rail, hair whipping in the wind, face beaded with spray, eyes closed. And his heart contracted in his chest.

"I've been living dangerously near the edge," he said to

her, because he felt she deserved at least that much honesty from him. "And creeping closer all the time."

"I know, Devon. I was frightened for you."

"But you came to me. I'll never understand how...or why, but you did. And somehow, Enya, you gave me back my soul."

"It was never really gone. You only needed a bit of a nudge to help you see it again."

He nodded, wondering—and not for the fist time—how a woman so young could seem to possess the wisdom of the ages. "You helped me find peace," he said. "And I'll always be grateful for that." She looked at him, smiling in that serene way she had, making him feel guilty as hell for taking so much and giving so little.

"I owe you. I really do. I only wish I could give you what you need from me."

Her chin lowered fractionally. "You mustn't feel guilty for that, Devon. You can't force yourself to feel something that isn't in your heart. Even if you tried, it would never pass. You couldn't even fool me with such a farce, to say nothing of...anyone else."

He frowned at the hesitation, felt like a monster. "I care for you, Enya. And God knows...I want you."

Her head came up sharply, eyes sparkling with liquid fire for the briefest instant before she bit her lip and looked away. "It wouldn't be right," she whispered. "You don't love me."

He closed his eyes in anguish. "It's just too soon. If you could stay, give me a chance to get used to this new peace that I'm feeling...I've been living too long with the idea that I'd never love anyone. I can't just leap from that to undying devotion overnight. We've only had two days—"

"You know that's not true. We've had a good deal more." A tear shimmered on her lower lashes, but she rapidly blinked it away. "No matter. If you don't love me now, you never will. And even if you might, my time is nearly up. Tomorrow at midnight I'll be gone." She came to him, lifted one hand to cup his cheek. "But I must tell you, Devon MacKenzie, that I've not one regret. If my coming here has helped your broken heart to heal, then it was well worth the price o' the trip."

She stood on tiptoe, and very gently brushed her lips across his. And when she stepped away, her tears had finally spilled over.

"What price?" he asked her, skimming her cheeks with his fingertips, absorbing her tears into his skin. "What did you mean by that?"

She only smiled and shook her head "I thought we came out here to enjoy the sea, and not to talk on such dire matters as my leavin'. Let's float awhile, and look at the stars, and forget who we are."

Devon nodded, and turned to furl the sail while Enya dropped anchor. And then he sat in the boat's cushioned stern bench, and she sat close beside him. Her scent caressed him. Her hair tickled his cheek when the wind blew. He slipped an arm around her shoulders, and she relaxed against him, closing her eyes. His arm tightened around her. Her head fell gently to his shoulder. Turning just slightly, he pressed a kiss to her forehead, and then he thought, what the hell, and turned still more, hooked a finger beneath her chin, lifted her face and fitted his mouth over hers. He kissed her, and something kicked his heart into overdrive the second he touched her lips with his own. But there was no response. It was only when he lifted his face away that he realized why. Enya had fallen asleep.

Water awakened her. Tiny droplets of it, splattering on her face in time with the rocking motion. Not the rocking motion of the sea. Nor were these droplets like the ocean's warm kisses. This was different. Colder and less dense, wetting her skin, her arms where they were linked around....

She opened her eyes to look straight up into Devon's face, wet with raindrops like her own. And her arms were linked around his neck, and his were holding her firmly. He was carrying her. Carrying her along a jagged, rocky bit of shoreline, higher and higher, away from the sea. A rumble of thunder muttered in the sky. A flash of lightning, and the rain came harder.

"Where are we, Devon? What's—"

He looked down at her, gave her a reassuring smile. "It's all right. You fell asleep on the boat, and I got so wrapped up in sailing, I lost track of the time. I saw the storm clouds rolling in and decided we'd better come ashore to wait it out. Too far to go back home."

The wind picked up. Devon stopped walking and set Enya on her feet. "I see lights in the distance." He pointed. "Let's hurry. We can get to a phone and—"

"But why?"

Enya tipped her head back, letting the strengthening rainfall pummel her face, feeling the wind caress her. Standing perfectly still, arms out at her sides.

"Enya, what the hell are you doing?"

*"Feelin', Devon."*

"You're going to catch your death."

She almost laughed aloud when he said that. Death was something she couldn't help but catch. Not tonight, though. Tonight, she was alive. And she would enjoy every minute of it. And tomorrow, well, it would be what it would be. If she died, then it must be her time.

"Enya, come on."

"No." She opened her eyes and looked around her, smiling when she spotted the perfect spot from which to enjoy the storm, to fully relish the magnificence of nature. "You go on," she told Devon. "Go find shelter, dry yourself off. When the storm passes, I'll be right up there." And without giving him another glance, she ran from him, clambering up the stony slope to the large flat ledge that protruded out over the sea. When she reached that ledge, she stood upon its very lip, arms outspread, facing the storm that rolled in from the sea. She wanted to feel everything she could before tomorrow night when she would feel no more.

Devon's hands closed on her shoulders from behind. "Enya," he whispered.

And she turned to him, looked at him. His raven hair, plastered to his forehead, streams of water running from it, down over his face and his corded neck. Raindrops beaded on the soft curling hairs of his forearms. The water purled on the skin of his chest, where his soaking wet shirt was open just a bit. She felt his body's heat. She smelled him. And she realized all over again that she had only one more day to live. *To feel*

"I'm sorry, Devon," she whispered. "I know it's terribly wrong."

"What is?"

She didn't answer. Instead, she curled her hands around the nape of his rain soaked neck, and she kissed him. Not the gentle, timid kiss she'd given him before, in the boat. A real kiss. A woman's kiss. Devon's response was swift and sure. His arms encircled her waist like satin chains, pulling her body hard and tight against his own. A deep moan seemed torn from the depths of him. And Enya felt a fire she'd never felt before. Heat sizzled through every part of her that he touched, and then engulfed her utterly.

Devon's mouth left hers to trail a warm path over her jaw, down to her throat and suckled her there, as if hungry for the taste of her skin.

"Aye, Devon," she whispered, though her voice had

become coarse and raspy. "Aye, it might be wrong. But it doesn't have to mean anything. Just let me have this. Just this. Just ...this...."

He pushed the strap of her dress down over her shoulder, kissed her there, nipped her skin gently, playfully. And when he sank to his knees, he took her down with him.

# CHAPTER TEN

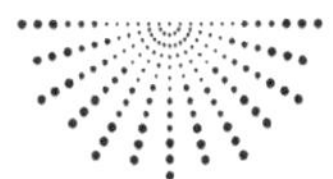

*The Ecstasy*

He was lost. The instant her arms twisted tight around his neck, the moment her mouth sought his, and the second she pressed closer, as if she felt this same strong yearning, he was lost. He'd wanted her this way from the moment she'd fainted in his arms after her boat broke apart in the tide. No, even before then. He'd wanted her this way since his own accident, when she'd kissed him on the beach just the way she was kissing him now. And deep inside, he knew he'd wanted her even longer than that. Maybe forever. Maybe even beyond forever.

His body responded to her in a way his heart could not. And that he'd denied these feelings release with everything in him, only made them stronger and more furious now that they'd broken free. He knelt, and she knelt, and he held her to his chest, and she pressed even closer. He plumbed her mouth, and she tilted her head and opened it wider. He kissed the rain-wet skin of her shoulders, where he'd already pushed the dress away. He pushed the material still further, sliding his palms down her slick arms, and pulling them free of the garment. It pooled around her knees, because it could fall no further.

Devon clasped the warm, soft skin of her waist, then slid his hands around to the small of her back. He ran his palms up her spine's enticing curve, and rubbed circles over her shoulders, and then leisurely slid them downward again until her buttocks filled his palms, and he could squeeze and massage and pull at them while feeding on her luscious mouth.

He felt her swift intakes of breath, the startled gasps that seemed to come each time he moved or touched in a new way. It set his heart to beating even faster and harder. He drew his hands around her body again, to the front of her, never breaking the contact as he did. He slid them between his chest and hers, and he captured her breasts. Her response was to shiver, and back away just slightly, giving him more room. She was breathless. He was relishing her. It had never been like this. Never. It was as if he could feel every ripple of pleasure he sent through her body.

He pressed her backward, and she went, lying down on

the cold stone. The clouds seemed to part and the storm came in torrents. Rain pummeled her face, and spattered off the rock around her body. He sat astride her, upright, watching in an unbearable agony of desire as the raindrops pounded down on her breasts and belly with little smacking sounds. And when he could bear the watching no longer, he bent his head to those succulent mounds, and drank every drop from one, and then the other. He sat up, never taking his eyes from her beautiful brown ones, he peeled off his wet shirt and kicked free of his jeans. And then he returned to her again, joining her there on their rain-soaked stone bed.

As soon as he lay down upon her, her arms locked around him, she kissed him desperately. Devon took his time, sensing her inexperience, knowing the same way he knew so many things about her—things he had no way of knowing, and yet knew, all the same.

The wet stone beneath his knees was cool and hard. The pounding rain beat down on his back and shoulders, icy cold. And her rain-kissed body, pressed tight to his, was warm everywhere they touched, and exquisitely soft. He felt as if his soul was falling into hers, and it was a beautiful place to be.

Later, as Devon let his head rest back against his stone pillow, Enya's rested upon is chest.

"I love rainstorms," she whispered. "Most of us do."

"Yeah," he said softly, with a brand new wonder dawning in his heart. "Yeah, so do I. I just never knew it until now."

Eventually, Devon walked to the nearest house and called a cab. While he waited for it, he secured the boat more thoroughly, hoping it would still be there in the morning, when he came back for it.

When he returned to the spot where he'd left her, Enya was sitting on the stone. She'd put on her soaking wet dress as if it was an everyday thing. Her knees were bent, her arms wrapped around them, and her heart stopping brown eyes were pensive and intense. He wondered what she was thinking about. He wasn't even sure he wanted to know. Because the look in her eyes...it scared him.

Something had happened between the two of them on this ledge tonight. Something that had never happened to him before. And he wished to God she would stick around long enough for him to find out exactly what it had been.

But she wouldn't. She'd made that clear.

He touched her shoulder. "Enya, there's a cab coming. It'll be here by the time we can walk down to the road."

She blinked and glanced up at him, her smile, very slight and wavering, and unspeakably sad. She got to her feet and walked at his side along the over a grassy meadow, and onto a path that led to the road, and she never said a word. Not a word. He didn't know if she regretted what they'd done tonight, or relished it. He didn't know whether she wished she'd never met him now or whether she'd changed her mind about leaving so soon. He didn't know anything.

In the back seat of the cab, she fell asleep. By the time they arrived home she was shivering. Goosebumps rose on her arms; he felt them when he touched her. And she was sleeping so soundly she didn't even stir when he scooped her out of the taxi and carried her into the house.

Belle stepped into his path, between the front door and the stairway. She wore a flannel nightgown and opened her mouth to ask what had happened, concern in her eyes.

But Devon spoke before she could. "Shshh. It's okay, Belle, she's only sleeping." He whispered the words. But his eyes were on the woman in his arms, not on the woman he spoke to. "We got caught in the rain," he explained, and his gaze skimmed the still damp column of her throat, and the place where the dress dipped low on her chest. His throat went dry. "But it's okay. I'll take care of her."

Belle muttered a reply, but he didn't hear what she said. He moved past her and up the stairs, easily carrying Enya to her room. He laid her on the bed, peeled the wet dress from her chilled body. He couldn't not look at her. He couldn't not notice that she was the most beautiful woman he'd ever known. And he *did* know her. He knew her as well as he knew himself, though how that could be possible was beyond comprehension. He'd always known her. He knew that her physical beauty was but a dim reflection of the beauty she held inside. Her heart, her soul, they were blinding in their beauty.

With a warm, fluffy towel, he gently rubbed her dry. And then he tucked her beneath the covers. Bending low, he kissed her forehead. There was a pang of regret that twisted his insides into knots when he turned to leave her.

It was so powerful that he turned back once more.

"I don't know, Enya," he whispered. "I don't know what this is...what *you* are. I don't know if I'm ready for it, and I damned well don't know what to do about it. I need time. Why can't you just give me some time?"

Pushing both hands through his hair, he forced himself to turn away, to stop thinking about crawling into that bed with her and pulling her into his arms. Dammit he'd gone too far. He knew what she wanted from him, and now she probably thought she was going to get it. She probably thought the tender way he'd made love to her tonight meant something...something more than it truly had.

He would have to make her understand that wasn't necessarily the case. He'd have to tell her. And that wasn't a blow he looked forward to delivering. He closed her bedroom door and moved down the hall to his own, lonely room.

He barely slept. She, on the other hand, slept as if comatose. He lingered in the house all morning, dreading the moment when she'd come down the stairs and look into his eyes and see the truth there. That it had been only physical. Passion, yes, there was incredible passion between them. But that was all. It had to be all. A man couldn't spend years incapable of feeling love, and then feel it overnight. Even a man with a normal, undamaged heart couldn't fall in love so quickly.

*But you've known her a lot longer than that.*

He ignored the voice in his mind, in his heart, and he waited for Enya to come downstairs. But she didn't come down. And Devon could no longer stand the tension building in him as he awaited the moment when he'd look into her eyes again. So like a coward, he ran. He could talk to Enya later. Much later.

"You're not leaving...?"

"Yeah, I am," he told Belle, wishing for once she'd mind her own business the way George had been doing all morning.

"But suppose she takes sick? She was soaked to the skin last night, Devon. She might have caught her death—"

"She didn't." He knew, too well, didn't he? Hadn't he crept into her room several times during the night, and at least twice this morning, just to check in on her? Just to run his hands over the satin skin of her face to check her temperature? There'd been no fever. No reason to worry. But he'd kept returning anyway. She was like a drug he couldn't resist

He had to get out of here. He couldn't think.

"I have to go get the boat," he explained to Belle. "I can't just leave her, Belle, or I'll go back and she'll be gone."

"Exactly," Belle said, scowling at him. "You'll get back and she'll be gone. And then what will you do?"

He frowned. "I'm talking about the boat and you know it. I spent months on her. She's worth—"

"She's priceless. Any stranger passing by could tell that

much. Any man with a heart would snap her up in a second."

He held Belle's gaze. She stared right back at him, eyes blazing until he finally looked down first. "I have to go, Belle." He turned to head out the door before she could say another word.

She slept like she'd never slept before. She barely remembered the ride back to Devon's house or the way he'd carried her up the stairs and tucked her into bed. She knew it had happened, but it had happened while she'd been asleep, contented, cozy, all wrapped in a soft pink glow. She'd never known love could be as it had been between the two of them. And while she knew he didn't love her, she had no regrets. She would have a precious memory to take with her when she left this life. And perhaps Devon would remember last night as well. Perhaps he'd think of her, and smile.

She came more fully awake, sat up in bed, and blinked at the brilliant sun shining down from high in the sky. "Lordy, it's so late!"

"Well, good morning, child. You look...rested."

She swung her gaze around, facing Belle, a bit self-consciously, she supposed. It was silly to think Belle could see everything that had happened last night just by looking into her eyes, but that was the way she felt. "I slept like the dead. But Belle, what time is it? It's my last day here, I cannot waste it lying about in bed!"

Belle smiled gently, and came further into the room. Enya noticed the tray she carried. "Nearly noon," she said, as she lowered the tray to Enya's lap. "But settle down. Here, have some breakfast. It will—"

"Oh, but I can't, Belle. You don't understand, it's my last day." She pushed at the tray so Belle couldn't set it down, and reached for the robe someone had left lying across the foot of the bed. "Where is Devon?" she asked. "I must talk to him."

Belle bit her lower lip and lowered her chin.

"What is it, Belle? Is Devon all right?"

"Of course he is, darling. It's just that...well, he had to leave."

Enya blinked in response to what felt like a blow. "He...he's gone?"

"Oh, he waited around as long as he could. I know he wants to see you. But he was concerned about leaving the boat unattended so long. So he went off to bring it home. He'll be back soon, though. Don't worry your head about that."

A sick feeling took shape in the pit of Enya's stomach. She battled a wave of tears, though they made no sense. It wouldn't take more than a few hours for Devon to go retrieve the boat, and bring it back home again, surely.

So why was she feeling such a bleakness of the soul? Such a certainty that this was it...over. The end.

"Here, Enya. Please, try to eat."

"No. Thank you all the same, Belle, but I...I've no appetite."

Belle frowned hard, but took the tray away. Shaking her head and muttering to herself, she left Enya alone.

Enya blinked and swallowed hard. She would be gone at midnight. Devon knew that. How could he leave her on her last day here? Especially after last night, and....

Oh. Well, maybe that was it. He was realizing what he'd done last night and maybe thinking she'd have expectations of him now. Perhaps he thought she'd be awaiting his declaration of undying love, and this was his way of avoiding her. He didn't want to have to look her in the face when he told her that it wasn't forthcoming, that last night had meant nothing to him. That he still didn't love her.

Lord, what a fool. She already knew all that. She hadn't expected one night of passion to change the man's heart. She'd wanted to know physical love just once, and only with him, before she died. But she couldn't very well have told him that, could she?

No. So now he had everything mixed up, and thought he had to avoid her. And she'd end up spending her last day in this world all alone. She battled her tears, but they came anyway. So she turned her face into her pillow, and she cried.

# CHAPTER ELEVEN

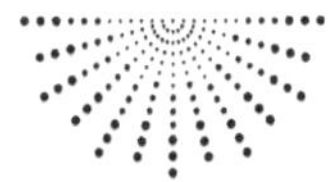

*The Revelation*

The further he drove, the more certain he was that he was making a terrible mistake. Stupid notion, that. He could get to the boat in a couple of hours, have it loaded on the trailer within a third, and make it back home two hours after that. Five hours. He'd be back home by dinnertime.

He was a jackass, wasting five hours away from her on her last day. But, dammit, he needed to be away from her. He couldn't think straight when he was looking into those velvety brown eyes. His mind got all clouded with emotions and longings, and practical wisdom took a back seat to passion.

So, the way he saw it, he was doing the only thing he could do. Hell, it wouldn't be any good at all to wait and do his soul searching after she left. Suppose he decided there was something there after all, and then couldn't find her again? No, he had to sort his feelings out before she left. And he had to do it alone.

The drive down the coast didn't do a hell of a lot to clear his mind, though. All he kept doing was picturing her face. Wondering if she was hurt that he'd skipped out before she'd awakened this morning. Wondering if she thought he hadn't wanted to see her again. He should have left her a note, explaining why he had to go.

And when he wasn't thinking about that, he was remembering every nuance of her, the way she'd been in his arms. The way she felt when he touched her. Her desire for him. A bit mind-boggling when he thought about that. A woman like her, burning for *him.* He remembered the way she'd sounded. Those little cries that seemed to come from the depths of her soul. The ones he'd learned just how to instigate. A touch here, a kiss there. Those cries were like music. Like angels singing. He wanted to hear them again. And there was the way she'd tasted, like drugged honey. Some sweet nectar he couldn't believe he craved now the way he did. And, God in heaven, the way she'd looked! Eyes passion-glazed, mesmerizing. Long, curling auburn & sable hair, dark with moisture and plastered to her face and her shoulders. Her lips, parted and inviting. The way the raindrops beaded on her skin.

He nearly hit a stop sign, and jerked the wheel to the left just in time to avoid it. Only he jerked a bit too hard, and slammed the brakes when he shouldn't have. He smelled hot rubber, heard the tires squealing and saw the trailer swinging up beside him like a jackknife folding together. He skidded sideways, wrenched the wheel into the skid, but it was too late. He felt the cessation of friction when the vehicle became airborne. The bone-jarring impact when it became earthbound again. And then he was rolling, rolling, rolling, his body being hammered, pummeled, slammed into one hard barrier after another. And then he sank into darkness. The last coherent thought he had, was of Enya.

She went swimming. She built a sand castle. She listened to music on the portable radio George had loaned her, and she had her first slice of pizza for lunch. She walked. She sat. She thought...about Devon. She was pretty sure she'd helped him to get past the guilt he'd been suffering since his brother's death. For that she was grateful. This whole adventure was worthwhile if Devon could just go on with his life.

She decided to write a letter to him, explaining everything. She had promised him she would tell him the truth before she left him, and as the hours sped past and early afternoon became late afternoon, and late afternoon became evening, she realized that he might not make it back in time for her to tell him in person. So this letter might be the only way. She spent a long time on the letter. She described the isle where she'd come from, and told-him all about the kinds of people who lived there. She told him all about the beautiful Fay Queen who was said to know all, and who'd refused to use her magic to help Enya become mortal. She told him about her deal with the ugly troll, and how she'd given away her wings and her in exchange for three days with Devon. And then she told him that she loved him, and that she had not one regret. She'd traded a lifetime for a few days with him, and given the chance, she would do so again. And she asked him to please find a way to be happy now that he knew his brother was all right.

She lowered the pen to the desk in her room, drained. She had no more to say. She'd poured every feeling, every emotion into the letter. It was done. She looked up from the sheet of lined paper, through the window at the darkened, star-dotted sky above, and she knew this would be the last star-gazing she would ever do.

She lifted her chin, resolved to face whatever awaited her without fear, and she took the note into Devon's bedroom. She laid it upon his pillow, then lowered her palm to the spot where his head would rest later, as if she could feel him there.

A jolt shot through her palm, up her arm straight to her heart, and her eyes widened. "Something's wrong," she whispered. "Sweet Mercy, something's terribly wrong."

She turned and ran from the bedroom, sick at heart, shouting to George and Belle as she raced down the stairs. "We must go after Devon," she cried. "Something's happened to him! I feel it in my bones."

Devon came around to see stars dotting the sky above him. Gradually pain came creeping in on the heels of consciousness, until he was fully awake, and in agony. Every part of him from the waist up, screamed in pain. He couldn't move. He could barely breathe. The car lay tilted on its side, neatly across his midsection. He couldn't feel his legs...nothing below the waist, which might be a blessing, when he thought about what he might be feeling if he *could* feel.

Dammit, what time was it? How long had he been lying there? Was it too late? Was Enya already gone? The thought of losing her this way, before he'd even made sense of his feelings for her, was as painful as the knife-sharp hurts raging through his body. Dammit, it couldn't end...not like this.

But it could. A glimpse of the lopsided, waning moon told him that it was nearing midnight. He would never make it back to her in time. He'd lost her. And having lost her, his mind cleared and his feelings became perfectly understandable to him. He grimaced in a pain even worse than his physical agony. Why had he been such an idiot?

A light flared in his eyes, and then there was a shout. Her shout. Enya's voice, floating to him through the barren night like an Irish blessing.

"Devon! Devon, where are you?"

"Here," he called out, and even as she ran closer he wondered if he was dreaming...or hallucinating. Until she dropped to her knees beside him, sobbing enough to break a heart, kissing his face and wetting it with her tears.

"My darlin' Devon... How badly are you hurt? Are you—"

"I love you!" He summoned every ounce of his strength and put all of it behind those words, so they emerged as a shout. "I love you, Enya. I want you to know that, in case—"

"In case nothing, you stubborn man. You're going to be fine."

"No. No, I'm not," he said real softly. He tried to touch her cheek, but couldn't feel his hand when he did. "I've been lying here with a car on top of me, and all I could think about was you, and that I didn't realize it soon enough. That I didn't tell you, and now it was too late. You would leave me–"

"Ah, but I don't have to leave you now, Devon. Not if you love me. Not if your love is true." She stroked his face, his hair. "I'll become mortal now. I'll be able to stay with you, my love."

He blinked. She couldn't stay with him. He was dying.

And he didn't know what the hell she meant...okay, part of him knew. But it was so farfetched....

"I kept to the rules, Devon. I didn't once use my magic, for if I had, I'd have died. And I never told you the conditions of the deal I made. And you love me all the same, and..." A frown creased her brows as she stared down at him. "Devon?"

He swallowed hard. "I'm sorry, angel. I...I can't...hold on...much longer..."

Her eyes widened. She shouted in the direction of the road, far above. "Belle! George! Where is the ambulance?"

"On the way," came the answering echo. "Fifteen minutes! Is he all right?"

Enya didn't answer. She pressed her hands to either side of Devon's face, and closed her eyes. "No," she whispered. "My sweet sweet love, you're dying. You're dying."

"I love you," he whispered, and he knew he wouldn't draw too many more breaths. "I'm sorry it took...me so long..."

He lifted a hand toward her. Weakly. But she didn't take it. Instead she rose to her feet. She stood above him, straight and strong, and the wind suddenly picked up strength. Her hair sailed out behind her and her dress snapped and billowed. "I'll not allow it!"

He frowned, staring up at her, wondering who it was she was shouting at. She stood with feet planted shoulder width apart, and lifted her arms to the sky. "If the price of using magic in this realm is death, then so be it!" she yelled. "Better my death than his!"

The wind whipped harder, blasting gusts of hurricane proportions down into the valley where he and his car had landed.

"Enya," he whispered. "What are you—"

"Ancient Gnomes of Mother Earth, lend me your strength," she said, her voice deep and resonant and commanding. Her eyes closed. She couldn't see, Devon thought, the way the wind was suddenly launching spirals of brown dirt all around him, around her.

"Sylphs of Air, grant me wisdom," she said, and the wind currents changed, seemed to become a whirlwind with Enya at their center.

"Undines of the Water, lend me your power!" Before Devon's eyes, clouds skittered over the moon, and within seconds a gentle rain began falling. And it seemed to Devon that it only fell here, in this gully, and nowhere else.

"Dancing Salamanders of Fire, grant me your passion!" Lightning split the sky, nearly blinding him.

Devon laid there on the ground while the elements seemed to join forces. The rain and wind, the dust and lightning, all swirling around Enya in a clockwise circle, and he knew he must be dreaming.

But hadn't she said she would die if she used magic?

"Burden, remove thyself from this man! Injuries, be gone! As I will it, so shall it be!" As she spoke, her eyes flew open and her arms swung downward, straight and so stiff they trembled, fingers pointing straight at him.

And he had to be hallucinating, because the wind and the dirt and the rain and the flashes of lighting seemed to blend together into one blur. A rainbow flash, green, yellow, red, and blue, dazzled him as it seemed to rush from her fingertips to engulf him. The car that laid on him vibrated, and suddenly became lighter. He blinked in shock as it hovered briefly above his body, then moved off to one side and crashed to the ground again. But the laser show wasn't over yet, because those light beams engulfed *him* now. And the feeling was coming back into his hips and his legs, even as the pain faded from the rest of his body.

And then the light retracted back into her fingertips. Enya sank to the ground as limp as a rag doll, whispering something he couldn't make out. Words of thanks or something. The wind died and the rain stopped, the lightning vanished and the dust settled. He tried to sit up, and it worked. Tried to stand, and found he could. No problem. Nothing even hurt. He shook off the shock of that, and forced his eyes to stay away from the ton or two of scrap metal this tiny bit of a woman had somehow lifted off his body. He went to Enya. He gathered her up into his arms and he held her, scooping her right off her feet, and he kissed her, thanked her.

"Enya, angel, you're so weak! You're shaking."

"Only because it was such big magic, Devon. I've never had call to harness quite so much power before."

"But..."

She lifted a hand to his cheek, caressed him there. "I'm of the fay, Devon. A fairy. I could become mortal only if you fell in love with me, and you did. But I broke the rules I agreed to. I used my magic, and now I'll pay the price. But I've no regrets, my love. No regrets at all, excepting that we hadn't more time together before I had to leave you."

He closed his eyes, held her tighter. "No. No, dammit, you didn't give your life to save mine! Tell me you didn't."

But she only closed her eyes to prevent her tears spilling over. "Enya, why?"

"Because I love you, Devon. More than life, I love you. Always have. Always will, darlin', wherever I am."

She lifted her head, kissed him. And he kissed her back, deeply, showing her everything he felt for her.

"I won't let it happen," he whispered. And then he tipped his head back, shouting at the sky. "Who the hell made these rules anyway! Take me! Dammit, let Enya live and take me!"

"No, Devon!"

A shimmering blue-green light appeared before him, and gradually took on form. In seconds a glowing woman stood there. Her hair was like spun gold, and her eyes gleamed exactly like twin diamonds, refracting rainbows of light that danced on everything they touched. Her gossamer wings, nearly transparent, moved gently in the breeze. Enya tugged at him, and Devon set her on her feet. She tucked her hand into his, and he immediately closed his around it. He wouldn't let her go, no matter what.

Enya bowed her head, and whispered, "Queen Ciarnan."

"Hello, Enya," the woman said, and her voice was like music.

"Majesty, I'm sorry I went against your wishes...but only sorry for the offense doing so caused you. I'd do nothing differently if I had the chance again."

"I know, child. And it's for that reason I've reached the decision I have."

Enya frowned, tilting her head. "I'm afraid it's too late for that, my lady. It was a terrible troll who gave me this chance, and it was to his terms I agreed. I broke the rules. I used my magic—"

"You willingly gave your life to save Devon's. And he only just now offered his own in exchange for yours."

"Aye," Enya said, lowering her head. "You've been watching, then."

"I'm always watching, Enya. Oh, child, I cannot grant whimsical wishes to every young fairy who fancies herself in love. I first must know that love is true. I would have been delinquent in my duties had I allowed you to give up your immortality and your magic, without first seeing proof that it was truly what was best for you."

Devon glanced at Enya, saw the puzzled expression she wore.

"I don't understand..."

The beautiful woman smiled. "I was the troll."

Enya gasped, her eyes going wide. "*You?*"

"I had to learn how strong your love for this mortal

was, and to see for myself the purity of his love for you. And my dear child, I find both to be worthy. More than worthy."

"You—you mean...?"

"Yes, Enya. You're mortal now. A human woman, with a mortal lifetime, to spend as you wish. Bright blessings, little one. I'll be watching over you, always."

The halo of light that surrounded the queen flared brighter, and then she was gone.

A siren wailed from the road high above, then stopped abruptly. Voices rose in a clamor, and then the sounds of tumbling rocks and dirt came as people made their way down the steep slope.

But Devon paid no attention. He was lost in sensation as he wrapped his delicate prize up in his arms and held her close. God, to think of how close he'd come to losing her! How very nearly he'd let this precious woman slip right through his fingers. Never again, he vowed, and he kissed her as if he'd never stop. Enya clung to him, smiling beneath his, kisses, and salting his lips with her happy tears.

The clambering footsteps halted close by.

"Merciful heavens," Belle whispered. "It's about time."

### The End

# Continue reading for an excerpt from
# ETERNITY,
# Book 1 of Maggie's EPIC series,
# THE IMMORTALS.

# EXCERPT: ETERNITY

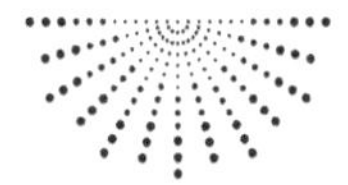

**She was executed for witchcraft. Death was only the beginning.**

Three hundred years ago, Raven St. James was hanged as a witch—and reborn as something far more powerful. An Immortal High Witch of the Light, Raven learns the truth too late: others survived as well. Dark witches who steal hearts to preserve their own eternal lives. And they are hunting her.

Duncan Wallace paid for loving Raven with his life.

Now, centuries later, he loves her again.

Haunted by memories that make no sense, Duncan is drawn to a woman who claims they shared a past life—and that she is immortal. He knows he should walk away. He knows it's impossible. But the pull between them is irresistible, and the danger stalking Raven is closer than either of them realize.

As ancient magic awakens and enemies close in, Raven and Duncan must face a terrifying truth: loving each other may doom them both…yet walking away could cost them everything.

# CHAPTER ONE

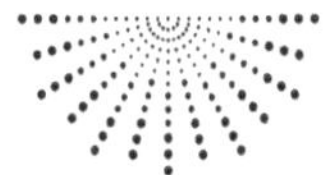

*I* always knew I was a witch.

The definition of the word has since broadened somewhat, and rightly so, I imagine. Today anyone with the determination to learn and practice the Craft of the Wise can call herself—and deservedly—a witch. But in my time there were no books written to guide a seeker, save the books of the witches themselves, but the grimoires were kept secret. Back then one was only a witch if one was born to, or adopted by, another witch. And even then the young one wasn't told all of the secrets. Some of them I didn't learn until much later.

My mother was a wise woman, a witch, and from the time I was very young I was taught the ways of drawing on the power of the sun and the moon and the stars and of nature itself. Above all else, I was taught the importance of keeping all that I learned secret. For the penalty meted out to practitioners of the Craft in those days was harsh.

Mother never told me just how harsh. I learned that when I was twenty and one, in a lesson so cruel its memory remains burned in my mind, though three full centuries have passed. And yet it was because of that cruelty that I first set eyes upon Duncan Wallace.

The key to my mother's ruin was her kindness. My father had died only a fortnight before, of a plague her simple folk magic could not fight. Many lives were lost in our small English village that brutal winter of 1689, and perhaps my mother simply could not bear to see one more death after so much grief.

At any rate, it was Matilda, the sister of my dead father, who came pounding on our door that dark wintry night. Looking startled at Aunt Matilda's state—wild hair and wilder eyes and not so much as a cloak about her shoulders—Mother drew her inside and bade her take the rocking chair beside the hearth to warm herself. I offered tea to calm her. But Aunt Matilda seemed crazed and refused to sit down. Instead, she paced in agitated strides, her skirts swishing about her legs, her thin slippers leaving damp footprints on our wood floor.

"No time to sit an' sip tea," she told us. "Not now. 'Tis my youngest, my little Johnny, named for my own dear brother who has gone to his reward. My Johnny has taken ill!" She whirled and grabbed my mother, gripping the front of her dress in white-knuckled fists. "I know you can help him. *I know*, I tell you! An' if you refuse me now, Lily St. James, I vow—"

"Matilda, calm yourself!" My mother's firm voice

quieted the woman, though only for a moment, I feared. "I would never refuse to help Johnny in any way I can. You know that."

"I *don't* know it!" my aunt shrieked. "Not when you let your own husband die of the same ailment! Pray, Lily, why didn't you save him? Why didn't you save my brother?"

My mother's head lowered, and I saw the pain flare anew in her eyes—a pain that sometimes dulled but never died away.

"I tried everything I knew to help Jonathon. But I couldn't save him," she whispered.

"Perhaps because you brought the illness on him from the start."

"Aunt Matilda!" I stepped between the two, forgetting to respect my elders and tugging my aunt's arm until she faced me, rather than my mother. "You know better. My parents shared a love such as few people ever know, and I'll not stand by and hear you sully its memory."

"Raven, don't," Mother began.

But I rushed on. "No one can bring on such a plague as this, and well you know it!"

"No one but a witch, you mean, don't you, Raven? *Raven.* She even named you for some dark carrion bird. Are you practicing the black arts as well, girl?" Aunt Matilda gripped my shoulders, shook me. "Are you? *Are you?*"

I could only blink in shock and stagger backward, pulling free of her chilled hands. My aunt *knew.* But how?

How could she know the secret that had been only between my mother and me? Even my father had been unaware....

"What makes you say such a thing?" my mother asked gently. "How can you accuse your own sister?"

"Sister-in-law and not by blood," Matilda reminded my mother. "And I know. I've always been suspicious of you and your Pagan ways, Lily. From the time you helped me birth my firstborn and somehow took away the pain. And later, when you nursed me through the influenza that should have killed me. You with your herbs and brews." She waved a hand at the drying herbs that hung upside down in bunches from our walls, and at the jars filled with philters and powders, lining the roughly hewn wooden shelves. "No physician could ease my suffering the way you did." She said it unkindly, made it an accusation.

Slowly my mother nodded, her serene expression never changing. "Herbs and plants are given by God, Matilda. Knowing how to use His gifts can surely be no sin."

"I saw you last full moon."

The words lay there, dropped like blows, as we stared at one another, my mother and I, both remembering our ritual beneath the full moon, when we chanted sacred words 'round a balefire at midnight.

"I know you have...powers. And I don't care if they're sinful or not. Not now. I need you to help Johnny. If you didn't conjure this plague, then prove it. Cure him, Lily. If you refuse...." Her eyes narrowed, but she didn't finish.

"If I refuse, you'll do what, dear sister? Bear witness against me to the magistrate? See me tried for witchery?"

Matilda didn't answer. She didn't need to. I saw her answer in her eyes, and my mother saw it as well.

"You've no need of such threats," Mother told her. "All you had to do was ask for my help. I'll try my best for your son, just as I did for Jonathon. But witchery or no, I may not be strong enough to help him."

"If he dies, I vow, I'll see you hang!" Aunt Matilda lurched toward the plank door, tugging it open on its rawhide hinges. "Gather what you need and come at once. I must make haste back to his bedside."

She left us in a swirl of snow, not bothering to close the door. I went and shut out the weather, then stood for a long moment, my hand on the door. I had a terrible premonition that the events of the past few moments would somehow change our lives forever. I didn't know how, or why, but I felt it to my bones. Drawing a deep breath, I turned to face my mother. I knelt before her, taking her hands in mine, staring up into eyes as black as my own. "Don't go to him," I begged her. "You cannot help him any more than you could help Father. And when he passes, she'll blame you."

"He is my own nephew," she whispered. She tugged her hands away, got to her feet, and began to make ready, taking sprigs of herbs from the dried bunches hanging on the wall, pouring a bit of this powder and a bit of that into her special cauldron. The one with the hand-painted red rose adorning its squat belly. She added steamy water from the larger cast-iron pot that hung in the fireplace to the brew.

"We should leave this village," I pleaded as I worked at her side, measuring, stirring, holding my hands above each concoction to push magical energy and healing light into it. "We should leave tonight, Mother. Our secret is known, and you've told me how dangerous that can be."

"I can't break my vows," she said. "You know that. When someone needs help, asks me for help, I am bound by oath and by blood to try. And try I will." She looked into my eyes. "You should pack a bag and go to London. Take the horse. Leave tonight. I'll send for you when—"

"I won't leave you to face this alone," I whispered, and I flung myself into her arms, stroking her raven hair, so like my own, though hers was knotted up in back while mine hung loose to my waist. "Don't ask me to, Mother."

Her mouth curved in the first smile I'd seen cross her lips since my father's death. "So strong," she said softly. "And always, so very stubborn. All right, then. Come, let us hasten to Johnny."

We quickly packed our potions and some crystals and candles into a bag, pulled our worn homespun cloaks over our heads and shoulders, and stepped out into the brutal winter's night.

But my cousin was dead before we even arrived at my aunt's house. And we were greeted by a wild-eyed woman who'd once claimed us as kin, and the group of citizens she'd roused from slumber, all bearing torches and shouting, "Arrest them! Arrest the witches!"

Cruel hands gripped my arms, even as I turned to flee. Accusations rang out in the night, and people stood round watching as my mother and I were surrounded, and then dragged over the frozen mud of the rutted streets. I cried out to my neighbors, begging for help, but none was forthcoming. And my heart turned cold with fear. As cold as the wind-driven snow that wet my face.

'Twas a long walk, the longest walk of my life. The poor shacks of the village fell away behind us as we were pulled and pushed along, and we emerged onto the cobbled streets that ran between the fine homes of the wealthy in the neighboring town. At last we stood before the house of the magistrate himself, trembling in the icy wind while our accusers pounded upon his door.

The man emerged in his nightclothes after a time, looking rumpled and irritated. "What's all this?" he demanded, white whiskers twitching.

"Two witches!" shouted the man who gripped my mother's arms tightly. The ones who brought this plague on us all, Honor."

The old man's eyes widened, then narrowed again as he perused us. Beyond him I could see the glow of a fire in a large hearth, and feel its heat on my face. I longed to go warm my hands by that fire. My fingers were already numb from the cold.

"What evidence have you against them?" the magistrate asked.

"The word of this one's own sister," said another, pointing at my mother.

"Matilda is not my sister," my mother said, her voice ever calm, despite the madness around her. I would never forget her face, beautiful and serene. Her eyes, so brave, no hint of fear in them. "She is the sister of my husband."

"Your husband who died of the plague!" the man cried out. "And now your nephew is taken as well."

"Many have been lost to the plague, sir. Surely you wouldn't accuse every bereaved family of witchery?"

The man glared at my mother. "Matilda St. James bears witness, Honor. She's seen them practicing their dark rites with her own eyes."

"'Tis a lie!" I shouted. "My aunt is maddened with grief! She knows not what she says!"

"Silence." The magistrate's command sent shivers down my spine. He stepped forward, glancing down at the woven sack my mother still clutched in her hands. "What have you there, woman?"

Mother lifted her chin, meeting his gaze. I could see the thoughts moving behind his eyes, the way he looked at us, judging us, though we were strangers to him.

"'Tis only some herbs," she said softly, "brewed in a tea."

"She lies," the man said. "Matilda St. James said this woman was bringing a potion to cure her young son. But she feared the witch would deliberately wait until it was too late to help the lad, and her fear proved true. A witch's brew lies in that sack, Honor. Nothing less, I vow."

"'Tis no potion nor brew," my mother told him. "'Tis simply some medicinal tea, I tell you."

"Are you a physician, wench?" the magistrate demanded.

"You know that I am not."

"Give me the sack."

The hands holding my mother's arms eased their grip, and she gave her sack over. The magistrate opened it, pawing its contents, and I shuddered recalling the stones we'd put inside. Glittering amethyst and deep blue lapis, for healing. And the candles, made by our own hands and carved with magical symbols to aid in Johnny's recovery. We would have set them around his bed, where they would have burned all night to protect him from the ravages of the plague.

The magistrate saw all of this, and when he looked up again, his eyes had gone cold. So cold I felt even more chilled despite the warmth from the fire at his back. "Put them in the stocks. We try them on the morrow. Perhaps a night in the square will convince them to confess and save us the time." He withdrew, leaving the door wide, and reappeared a moment later with a large key, which he handed over to one of the men. "See to it."

"No!" I cried. "You mustn't do this! We've done nothing wrong. Magistrate, please, I beg of you—"

His door closed on my pleas, and again I was pulled and dragged as I fought my captors. But my struggles were to no avail. And soon I found myself being forced to bend forward, my wrists and my neck pressed awkwardly into the stock's evil embrace. The heavy, wooden top piece was lowered as my own neighbors held me fast, and I heard the chain and the lock snapping tight.

I could not move. Could not see my mother, but I knew she was nearby, for I heard her voice, strained now, but steady. "Tell the magistrate he shall have my confession," she said. "But only if he will let my daughter go free. She knows nothing of this matter. Nothing at all. You must tell him."

The man to whom she spoke only grunted in reply. And then the villagers left us. In the town square, bent and held fast, we waited in silence for the dawn. The freezing wind cut like a razor, and the wet snow continued to slash at us. I shivered and began to cry, my face stinging with cold, my hands numb with it, my feet throbbing and swelling.

And then I heard my mother's gentle voice, chanting softly, "Sacred North wind, do us no harm. Ancient South wind, come, keep us warm." Over and over she repeated the words, and I forced my teeth to stop chattering and joined with her, closing my eyes and calling to the winds for aid. My mother's folk magic could not make iron chains melt away. But she could invoke the elements to do our bidding.

Within minutes the harsh wind gentled, and the snow stopped falling. A warmer breeze came to replace the bitter cold, and my shivering eased. I was still far from comfortable, bent this way, unable to relieve the ache in my back. But I knew my mother must be suffering far more than I, for her body was older than mine. Yet she did not complain. I took strength from that, and vowed to keep my discomfort to myself.

"Hard times await us, my daughter," she told me. "But whatever happens tomorrow, Raven, you must remember what I tell you now. Promise me you will."

"I promise," I whispered. "But, Mother, you mustn't confess anything to them. Not even to save me. I couldn't live if you were to die." The thought terrified me, and I pulled my hands against the rough wood that held them prisoner, though I could not hope to work them free. She was all I had in this world. All I had.

"Perhaps this is my destiny," she said softly. "But 'tis not yours."

"How can you know that?"

"I know," she whispered. "I've known from the day you were born, child. By the birthmark you bear upon your right hip. The crescent." Tears burned my eyes. But my mother went on. "You're a far more powerful witch than I have ever been, Raven."

"No. 'Tis not true. I can barely cast a decent circle."

She laughed then, softly, and the sound of it touched my heart. That she could laugh at a time like this only made me love and respect her more than I already did, though I'd never have thought it possible.

"I speak not of the form of ritual, but the force, Raven. The power is strong in you. And you will need that strength. When this is over, child, you must leave here. Go to the New World. My sister, Eleanor, is there, in a township called Sanctuary, in the colony of Massachusetts. She is not a witch, and knows nothing of our ways. She was born of my father's faithlessness and raised by her own mother and not in our household. But she is kind. She will not turn you away."

"Perhaps not," I said. "But *I* will not leave you behind."

"I fear 'tis I who will leave you behind, my darling. 'Tis the night of the dark moon, when our powers ebb low. But even were our lady of the moon shining her full light down upon us, I doubt I could save myself. Do not cry for me, Raven. Dying is part of living, a birth into a new life. You know this."

"Oh, Mother, stop saying such things!" I cried loudly, sobbing and choking on my tears.

When Mother spoke again, I could hear tears in her voice as well. "Raven, listen to me. You must listen."

I tried to quiet myself, to do as she wished, but I vowed she would not die tomorrow. Somehow I would save her.

"When 'tis over," she told me, "you must return to our cottage in the village. But do so by night, and be very careful. You mustn't be seen. Do not wait too long, child, lest they burn the house in their vengeance or award it to Matilda's family in return for her testimony against us. You must go back in secret. Gather only what you will need for your journey. Then go to the hearth. There is a loose stone there. Take what you find hidden beyond that stone."

"But, Mother—"

"And take the horse, if she is still there. You may sell her in some other village. But take care. Should you meet anyone, do not tell them your true name. And as soon as you can, book passage on a ship to the New World. Now promise me you will do these things."

"I'll not let them kill you, Mother."

"There is nothing you can do to prevent it, child. I'll have your promise, though, and I will die in peace because of it. Promise me, Raven."

Sniffling, I muttered, "I promise."

"Good." She sighed, so deeply it seemed as if some great burden had been lifted from her shoulders. "Good," she whispered once more, and then she rested. Slept, perhaps. I could not be sure. I cried in silence from then on, not wishing to trouble my Mother with my tears. But I think she knew.

When dawn came, it brought with it the magistrate, and beside him a woman, looking distraught with red-rimmed eyes. Behind them walked a man who wore the robes of a priest. He had an aged face, thin and harsh, with a hooked nose that made me think of a hawk, or some other hungering bird of prey. He was pale, as if he were ill, or weak. And then they came closer, and I could see only their feet, for I could not tip my head back enough to see more.

"Lily St. James," the Magistrate said, "you and your daughter are charged with the crime of witchcraft. Will you confess to your crimes?"

My mother's voice was weaker now, and I could hear the pain in it. "I will confess only if you release my daughter. She is guilty of nothing."

"No," the woman said in a shrill voice. "You must execute them now, Hiram. Both of them!"

"But the law—" he began.

"The law! What care do you have for the law when our own child has become ill overnight? What more proof do you need?"

At her words my heart fell. She blamed us for her child's illness, just as my aunt had done. No one could save us now.

I heard footsteps then, and sensed the magistrate had gone closer to my mother. Leaning over her, he said, "Lift this curse, woman. Lift it now, I beg of you."

"I have brought no curse upon you, nor your family, sir," my mother told him. "Were it in my power to help your child, I would gladly do so. As I would have for my own husband and for my nephew. But I cannot."

"Execute them!" his wife shouted. "Michael was fine until you arrested these two! They brought this curse on him, made him ill out of pure vengeance, I tell you, and if they live long enough to kill him, they will! Execute them, husband. 'Tis the only way to save our son!"

The priest stepped forward then, his black robes hanging heavily about his feet and dragging through the wet snow. His steps were slow, as if they cost him a great effort. He went first to my mother, saying nothing, and I could not see what he did. But he came seconds later to me and closed his hand briefly around mine.

A surge of something, a crackling, shocking sensation

jolted my hand and sizzled into my forearm, startling me so that I cried out.

"Do not harm my daughter!" my mother shouted.

The priest took his hand away, and the odd sensation vanished with his touch, leaving me shaken and confused. What had it been?

"I fear you are right," the priest said to the magistrate and his wife. "They must die, or your son surely will. And I fear there is no time for a trial. But God will forgive you that."

Pacing away, his back to us, the magistrate muttered, "Then I have little choice." And the three of them left us alone again. But only for a few brief moments.

"Mother," I whispered. "I'm so afraid."

"You've nothing to fear from them, Raven."

But I *did* fear. I'd never *felt* such fear grip me as I felt then, for within moments the priest had returned, and he brought several others with him. Large, strong men. People filled the streets as my mother and I were taken from the stocks. The people shouted and called us murderers and more. They threw things at us. Refuse and rotten food, even as the men bound our hands behind our backs and tossed us onto a rickety wagon, pulled by a single horse. I crawled close to my mother, where she sat straight and proud in that wagon, and I leaned against her, my head on her shoulder, my arms straining at their bonds, but unable to embrace her.

"Be strong," she told me. "Be brave, Raven. Don't let them see you tremble in fear before them."

"I am trying," I whispered.

The wagon drew to a stop, and the ride had been all too short. I looked up to see a gallows, one used so often it looked to be a permanent fixture here. I was dragged from the wagon, and my mother behind me. But she didn't fight as I did. She got to her feet and held her head high, and no one needed to force her up the wood steps to the platform, while I kicked and bit and thrashed against the hands of my captors.

She paused on those steps and looked back at me, caught my eyes, and sent a silent message. *Dignity.* She mouthed the word. And I stopped fighting. I tried to emulate her courage, her dignity, as I was marched up the steps to stand beside her, beneath a dangling noose. Someone lowered the rough rope around my neck and pulled it tight, and I struggled to be brave and strong, as she'd so often told me I was. But I knew I was trembling visibly, despite the warmth of the morning sun on my back, and I could not stop my tears.

That priest whose touch had so jolted me stood on the platform as well, old and stern-faced, his eyes all but gleaming beneath their film of ill health as he stared at me...as if in anticipation. Beside him stood another man who also wore the robes of clergy. This one was very young, my age, or perhaps a few years my elder. In his eyes there was no eagerness, no joy. Only horror, pure and undisguised. They were brown, his eyes, and they met mine and held them. I stared back at him, and he didn't look away, but held my gaze, searching my eyes while his own registered surprise, confusion. I felt something indescribable pass between us. Something that had no place here, amid this violence and hatred. It was as if we touched, but did so without touching. A feeling of warmth flowed between him and me, one so real it was almost palpable. And I knew he felt it, too, by the slight widening of his eyes.

Then his gaze broke away as he turned to the older man and said, "Nathanial, surely 'tis no way to serve the Lord."

The kiss of Scotland whispered through his voice.

"You are young, Brother Duncan," the older man said. "And this no doubt seems harsh to you."

"What it seems like to me, Father Dearborne, is murder."

"'Thou shalt not suffer a witch to live,'" the priest quoted.

"'Thou shalt not kill,'" the young Scot—Duncan—replied. And he looked at me again. "They've nay been tried."

"They were tried in the square by the magistrate himself."

"It canna be legal."

"His Honor's own child is ill with the plague. Would you have us wait for the child to die?"

The young man's gaze roamed my face, though he spoke to the old one. I felt the touch of those eyes as surely as if he caressed me with his gentle hands, instead of just his gaze.

"I would have us show mercy," he said softly. "We've no proof these women have brought the plague."

"And no proof they haven't. Why take the risk? They are only witches."

The beautiful man looked at the older one sharply. They are human creatures just as we are, Nathanial." And he shook his head sadly. "What are their names?"

"Their names are unfit for a man of the cloth to utter. If you so pity them, Duncan, ease your conscience by praying for their souls. For what good it might do."

"'Tis wrong," Duncan declared urgently. "I'm sorry, Father, but I canna be party to this."

"Then leave, Duncan Wallace!" The priest thrust out a gnarled finger, pointing to the steps.

Duncan hurried toward them, but he paused as he passed close to me. Then turned to face me, as if drawn by some unseen force. His hand rose, hesitated, then touched my hair, smoothing it away from my forehead. His thumb rubbed softly o'er my cheek, absorbing the moisture there. "Could I help you, mistress, believe me I would."

"Should you try they would only kill you, as well." My voice trembled as I spoke. "I beg you...Duncan...." His eyes shot to mine when I spoke his name, and I think he caught his breath. "Do not surrender your life in vain."

He looked at me so intently it was as if he searched my very soul, and I thought I glimpsed a shimmer of tears in his eyes.

"I willna forget you," he whispered, then shook his head, blinked, and continued, "in my prayers."

"If there be memory in death, Duncan Wallace," I said, speaking plainly, even boldly, for what had I to lose now? "I shall remember you always."

He drew his fingertips across my cheek, and suddenly leaned close and pressed his lips to my forehead. Then he moved on, his black robes rustling as he hurried down the steps.

"Do you wish to confess your sins and beg the Lord's forgiveness?" the old priest asked my mother.

I saw her lift her chin. "'Tis you who ought to be begging your god's forgiveness, sir. Not I."

The priest glared at her, then turned to me. "And you?"

"I have done nothing wrong," I said loudly. "My soul is far less stained than the soul of one who would hang an innocent and claim to do it in the name of God." Then I looked down at the crowd below us. "And far less stained than the souls of those who would turn out to watch murder being done!"

The crowd of spectators went silent, and I saw Duncan stop in his tracks there on the ground below us. He turned slowly, looking up and straight into my eyes. "Nay," he said, his voice firm. "'Tis wrong, an' I willna allow it!" Then suddenly he lunged forward, toward the steps again. But the guard at the bottom caught him in burly arms and flung him to the ground. A crowd closed around him as he tried to get up, and he was blocked from my view. I prayed they would not harm him.

"Be damned, then," the old priest said, and he turned away.

The hangman came to place a hood over my mother's head, but she flinched away from it. "Look upon my face as you kill me, if you have the courage."

Snarling, the man tossed the hood to the floor and never offered one to me. He took his spot by the lever that would end our lives. And I looked below again to see Duncan there, struggling while three large men held him fast. I had no idea what he thought he could do to prevent our deaths, but it was obvious he'd tried. Was still trying.

"'Tis wrong! Dinna do this thing, Nathanial!" he shouted over and over, but his words fell on deaf ears.

"Take heart," my mother whispered. "You will see him again. And know this, my darling. I love you."

I turned to meet her loving eyes. And then the floor fell away from beneath my feet, and I plunged through it. I heard Duncan's anguished cry. Then the rope reached its end, and there was a sudden painful snap in my neck that made my head explode and my vision turn red. And then no more. Only darkness.

**Read more of *Eternity*.**

*Don't miss the rest of the books in the By Magic Series:*

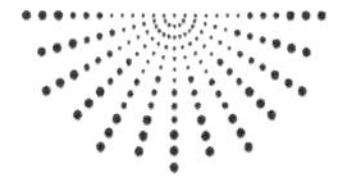

# CHAPTER TWO

*D*uncan didn't even know her name.

He didn't even *know her name.*

And yet he felt as if he'd lost a treasured friend—more than that, even. 'Twas as if a part of his own soul had just been brutally murdered in the town square.

Her surname, St. James, he'd heard that much muttered in the streets. More than that he did not know. Might never know.

"I tried," he whispered. "God knows I tried."

He'd been moved beyond all reason, all logic, when he'd heard her strong, deep voice and the courage it held as it rang out over the spectators, shaming them as they should well be shamed. And he'd known then that he had to try. Though he had no idea now what he could have done, even had they let him pass. Even had he reached her again. Perhaps he'd been a bit mad.

Perhaps she truly was a witch and had cast some spell,

some enchantment, o'er his heart there on the gallows. He didn't know. He only knew that something had possessed him—some sudden, violent, *desperate* need to save her.

And that he'd failed.

She swung slowly from the end of a rope beside her mother, her life snuffed out far too soon. And he realized, by the cold dampness seeping through his robes and chilling his legs, that he knelt now, before the gallows. He seemed to have fallen right where he'd been standing when the trapdoor had jerked away from beneath the beautiful girl. And he remained there still, kneeling in the snow.

He got to his feet, but his legs felt weak and his chest hollow. Staggering forward, he snatched a blade from a local man's belt as he passed the fellow. Ignoring the man's outcry, he moved beneath the gallows, to gather the young woman's body into his arms. He held her tight to him as he sawed at the rope until it gave way. Her weight fell upon him, head resting on his shoulder like a lover's. Satin soft hair, snow damp and fragrant, brushed against his cheek. He closed his arms around her body and turned his face full into that hair to inhale it and to feel it and to commit it to memory—as well as to hide the inexplicable tears that welled up in his eyes. So warm, her face on his skin. So much as if she were only sleeping.

"What might you have been to me?" he asked her, his voice a strangled whisper. "What might we have been to each other?"

But he spoke to death, and death did not answer.

"Though it makes no sense, lass, my heart is broken. I didna know you at all, an' yet it feels so very much as if I did. As if I always have." He rocked her in his arms, and a sob choked him. "Can you hear me? Are you out there, somewhere, listenin', lass? I'll give you a proper burial, I vow it. An' your dear mother, too."

He held her close, enveloped in a sadness he could not explain and a new certainty about the path he would walk in this life. And he owed her thanks for that, if nothing else, he realized.

A heavy hand fell upon his shoulder. "What sort of spectacle do you wish to make of yourself, boy?"

Duncan turned to see the murderer himself, Nathanial Dearborne, his own trusted mentor. "Do you ken what you've done this day?" he asked the man.

Nathanial's eyes narrowed, and he signaled to someone with a flick of his wrist. Immediately three men rushed forward to tear the beauty from Duncan's arms, as he cried out in protest. They bore her away, dumping her body on the back of a rickety wagon where her mother already lay. The man in the driver's seat snapped the reins, and the wagon trundled away.

"Where are they takin' her?" Duncan demanded, addressing Dearborne but keeping his gaze riveted to that wagon—to *her*—until it rounded a curve and disappeared from sight.

To the pit beyond the town. Best to get their kind as far from decent folk as possible, lad. You'll understand one day. This was for the best."

"'Twas murder," Duncan spat out, "an' sin of the most vile sort!" He glared at the man now that the wagon was gone from his sight. "I canna continue under the tutelage of a man who would condone it. My studies end here, today, Nathanial. I want no part of your priesthood, for you've shown it to be one of purest evil."

Nathanial's cloudy blue eyes narrowed, but not in anger, and he didn't shout "Blasphemy!" as Duncan had expected.

He simply said, "I'd hold my tongue, were I in your place, Duncan. You have no idea what sorts of forces you are dealing with."

"I willna hold my tongue. I *canna!*"

Nathanial shook his head slowly. "You know the teachings of the Church. The elimination of witches is our duty as Christians, Duncan. 'Tis imperative we wipe them from existence, rid the world of the scourge of witchery."

Duncan searched the old man's face. He'd been close to him once, thought of him almost as fondly as he did his own father. No more. "An' what will you do next, Nathanial, when you've murdered them all? What will your next mission be? To rid the world of anyone else whose beliefs differ from your own?"

Nathanial smiled. "The Crusades attempted that and failed. I simply seek to do my duty, Duncan. And 'twill be a service to all Christians if I succeed."

"Nay," Duncan said. "Not all." And he turned from the man, feeling nothing now but loathing for him—a man he'd once thought to be closer to God than anyone he'd known. But Duncan realized now that Nathanial was nothing. Less than nothing. A killer who seemed to enjoy his work.

"Where are you going?" Nathanial demanded. "Do not turn your back on me, boy! Answer my question!"

With a glance over his shoulder and an awareness of the people looking on, listening in, Duncan replied. "I'm goin' to gather my things, Nathanial. An' then I'm goin' to see those two women get a proper burial. After that, I only know I'll be goin' as far away from you an' your kind as I can. You are no man of God, but a hypocrite an' a killer, an' I canna abide bein' in the same village with you."

Then he continued on his way without another word, hearing the gasps and whispers of the townspeople as he passed.

It surprised him when a hand fell upon his shoulder. Stopping in his tracks, he didn't turn around. For he knew that gnarled old hand well.

"Duncan, wait," Nathanial said. "Perhaps I was too harsh. 'Tis obvious this morning's work has distressed you. But there is truly no need to take such drastic measures. Surely you do not mean to leave here—"

"Aye, Nathanial, that I do."

"You cannot!"

Frowning, Duncan turned. Nathanial composed himself, tempered his voice. "Duncan, you've been like a son to me. Believe me, boy, were this action not necessary, I'd never have—"

"But you did. 'Tis done, Nathanial, an' there's no undoin' it now."

Lowering his head, Nathanial drew a breath. "I am ill, Duncan. Surely you know that."

"Aye, I know it. I've seen you growin' weaker by degrees, an' wished to God I could do somethin' about it, Nathanial. But I canna help you. An' being ill, even facin' death itself doesna give you the right to go about hangin' innocents."

"I had no choice."

"An' I have no choice now," Duncan said. He turned away, having nothing more to say to the old man he'd once loved. But as he walked on, he heard Nathanial continue.

"'Tis because of the girl, is it? This is *her* doing."

Duncan kept walking.

"Damn her," Nathanial cried. "Damn her, she'll pay. I'll *make sure* she pays!"

"She's beyond your reach now, Nathanial."

"Oh, do not be so sure of that, my boy," Nathanial muttered.

Duncan turned then, to see the old man walking away. He did not know what Nathanial could have possibly meant by his words. But it did not matter. The lass was gone now. Dead, and Nathanial was as responsible as if he had pulled the lever himself. Duncan would never forgive the man.

He went to his stark room in the back of the church, to gather his meager possessions into a sack. He would never return here again; he'd meant what he'd said. This place had been his home for two years as he studied for the priesthood at Nathanial's feet. But that was over now.

What he had seen today—and what *he'd felt*—had changed him forever. He sensed it deep inside, though he had no idea how this change would manifest. He only knew he had to leave.

He only knew that the strange beauty had touched him, touched his heart, his soul, and his life, and that he would feel that touch for a long, long time to come.

Slinging his sack over his shoulder, he walked out again into the streets. People whispered and pointed as he passed. He didn't care. He would have liked a horse. It was a long walk to the place where they'd taken the girl and her mother. But he sensed it would be only the beginning of an even more distant journey. That the steps he took now were the first steps on the way to his destiny.

The darkness that descended on me when I reached the end of that rope was a temporary one.

I remember so clearly the sudden, desperate gasp I drew, the blinding flash of white light that stiffened my body and made me fling my head backward as I dragged in as much air as my lungs could contain. The rapidly fading pain in my neck and my head. And the shock I felt as I realized...I was still alive.

*I was alive!*

I blinked my eyes open and looked around me, and then my stomach lurched. 'Twas daylight, morning. Still early, I guessed. I lay upon the ground with the bodies of the dead strewn around me. The bodies of hanged criminals, and those taken by the disease plaguing the area. This was the pit they'd dug for this purpose. Every so often men would come here with shovels to cover over the dead, and ready the place for another layer of victims of the plague and the gallows. But I was not dead.

*I was not dead.*

I sat up slow, gagging at the stench of rotting flesh, and looked around me, frantically searching for my mother. I'd had no idea her magic was strong enough to save us from the gallows, but it must have been, for I was alive, and she...she.... No. Oh, no!

I found her, and my heart shattered. She lay still, her neck broken, her eyes open but no longer beautiful nor shining like onyx. They were already dulled by the filmy glaze of death.

"Mother! No, Mother, no!" I gathered her into my arms, sobbing, near hysteria as I held her close, and rocked her against me. "You can't be gone! You can't leave me this way. Why, Mother?" But she did not answer, and so I screamed my question again, to the earth and the sky and the corpses all around me. "Why am I still alive? Why do I live, and not my precious Mother? Why?" But I knew I would get no reply.

Not from the dead. Not from my mother. Her spirit no

longer lived in this body. She was gone. Gone, and I was alone.

Eventually I sat back and looked down at her poor body, an empty shell, yes, but even so 'twould not remain here in this vile place. Not while my heart still beat on.

Gently I lifted her in my arms. I was taller, larger than she. But even then it should not have been so easy to carry her. I thought perhaps 'twas my grief making me strong.

I made my way out of the pit and took my mother's body into the forest nearby. And there, I scooped away the snow, and scraped out a grave for her with no more than my two hands and a flat stone for a tool. My nails were split, my fingers bleeding and throbbing with cold when I finished, but I was beyond noticing the pain. I buried my beloved mother there, and then I lay upon her grave and cried.

When at last he reached the gruesome place of the dead, Duncan shuddered at the sight of the bodies strewn there. He pressed a handkerchief to his face, and even then the stench was sickening. And disease, too, hung on the very air here. One could smell it, almost feel it. Yet he searched for the dark beauty among the dead.

"Where are you?" he whispered as his gaze scanned the carrion. That she should be here in this filth even for a short time brought a fury more powerful than any he'd felt before surging through his veins. What was it about her that caused such reactions in him? Why did he care so deeply for a girl he did not even know?

"Duncan!" a voice called, and he turned. "Come away from there afore you take ill!"

At the rim of the pit a young man Duncan had called friend since they were lads together in Scotland sat astride his horse. Samuel MacPhearson leaned on the pommel, looking down at him.

"I'll nay go until I find them," he said.

"Well, you willna find them, my friend, for they be elsewhere. I searched myself only an hour ago. Arrived here faster by horse, I suppose, than you could by foot."

"Are you certain?" Duncan asked.

"Aye. I wouldna lie to you about this, Duncan. I can see 'tis important to you. Or she is. Did you know the lass?"

"Nay," Duncan said, making his way to the edge. "But it felt as if I did." When he began to climb up, Samuel dismounted and bent to offer a hand. Duncan got his footing at the top and brushed at his soiled clothes. Homespun, and barely fitting. But all he had, once he'd discarded the robes he no longer felt able to wear.

"Why were you looking for them, Samuel?" Duncan asked.

"Same reason as you, I'd guess. To bury them proper. I liked what was done no more than you did, Duncan." He looked out over the dead and grimaced. "I didna find them, though."

Duncan's heart twisted. "Where can they be?"

Samuel smiled, but 'twas bitter. "No doubt your friend

Dearborne would claim they used black magic to rise up an' walk away. But I suspect there's a far more simple solution. Some relative came for their bodies in secret. It happens, Duncan."

Duncan nodded but met Samuel's eyes. "Nathanial Dearborne is no friend of mine."

"He was here, you know."

Duncan frowned. "Nathanial? Here?"

"Aye, lookin' for those two women himself, I do believe. An' if he got here afore me, Duncan, he must have run his horse ragged the whole way. I meant to ask him why that was, but he beat a hasty retreat when he saw my approach."

The thought of that bastard laying his hands upon the girl set Duncan's teeth on edge. "He didna find them? You're certain of that?"

"Certain as I can be," Samuel said. "He seemed to be still searchin' when I arrived, and he had no bodies o'er his saddle when he galloped away."

"What could he want with them?"

"Nothing good, I'll warrant."

"The bastard."

Samuel's brows rose in twin arches. "Ah, so your great teacher is a bastard, now, is he?"

Duncan sighed, looking at the ground. "You were right about him all along, Samuel, an' I should've listened to you. Aye, he's a bastard, an' a killer, an' I told him as much."

"Indeed," Samuel said, slapping Duncan's shoulder.

"Half the town knows of it by now." He tilted his head to one side. "They're sayin' she bewitched you, Duncan. Stole your heart right there on the gallows."

Duncan lifted his head to meet his friend's eyes. "Perhaps she did," he whispered.

"Aye, I can see this has shaken you deeply."

"An' what's shakin' me more is that I willna know where she rests. Even that small comfort has been stolen from me. 'Twas wrong, what was done to her, Samuel."

Samuel nodded. "'Tis yet another reason I've decided to move on. I'm takin' Kathleen and leavin' this place. An' Duncan, my new bride an' I would be proud to have you come along with us."

Duncan searched Samuel's face. "Where will you go? Back to Scotland?"

"Across the sea, my friend. To the New World. They say 'tis far different there. Opportunity for every man. The rich an' the poor, livin' as equals."

Taking a deep breath, Duncan thought hard about saying yes. He'd heard talk of this New World, this America, where religious persecution, 'twas said, did not exist. Wild and new and exciting. The idea appealed. But he had matters to attend to. Responsibilities to uphold.

"I'd like nothin' better than to do just that, Samuel. But not now. I must first return to Scotland to face my father with what I've done."

Samuel shook his head. "Angus will be furious, no doubt. He paid Dearborne an' the Church a goodly sum to take you in for trainin'."

"And I'll repay every bit," Duncan vowed.

"After you've repaid the debt to your father, Duncan, what then?"

Duncan shrugged, looking off into the distance, seeking something he couldn't name. "I dinna know. In truth, I just dinna know."

Samuel slapped his shoulder. "If you decide to join us in America, my friend, just come along. We'll welcome you gladly."

"Thank you," Duncan said. "I just might, at that."

"I hope you will." Then Samuel frowned. "In the meantime, Duncan, I hope you'll put this day's doings behind you. You've a haunted look about your eyes that worries me."

"Haunted," Duncan muttered. "Aye, 'tis the way I feel. I think that bonny lass will be hauntin' me for some time to come, Samuel. An' I doubt—rather seriously doubt—there's any way on God's earth I can put her memory behind me. I'm not even certain I want to."

Hours passed as I lay weeping atop my mother's grave. And then the day itself waned as well. 'Twas night again before I could even think of leaving her, even wonder about what I was to do now. And 'twas then I recalled her words to me the night before. I had promised I would do as she asked. I had promised her. I must keep that promise. But first....

I dried my tears, tried to reach for the calmness necessary to do what must be done. I searched for that serene place inside me. My breathing deepened. My heartbeat slowed. In silence I pointed my forefinger at the ground and drew an invisible circle round my mother's resting place. And within that circle I sat, closed my eyes, and wished my dear mother goodbye.

For just a moment the wind whispered through the trees overhead in such a way that it seemed my mother's voice spoke to me. *Be strong, Raven. I am with you...always.*

"Mother?" Rising, I looked all around me, but saw nothing. Only the very thin sliver of the newborn moon appearing in the sky. Like a sign, to start anew. To find a way to go on.

'Twas what my mother would have wanted.

I brushed my fresh tears away and nodded. 'Twas time. But I did not close the circle I'd cast. I left it there, willing it to protect her unmarked grave from harm of any kind. That done, I forced myself to leave her there, so that I could begin doing what she'd asked of me.

I followed her instructions to the letter, sensing she might know, somehow, and be disappointed in me if I did not.

I went to our cabin under cover of darkness, and slipping inside I saw chaos. Our home had been stripped of anything we had of any value. Blankets and clothing, our copper and iron pots. Everything. Even my mother's precious cauldron, which I'd hoped to take with me that I might be reminded of her each time I brewed a magical potion or used it in ritual. She'd painted a tiny red rose upon its face. It had been her most cherished possession.

But it was gone now.

Something glittered up at me from the floor, and I bent to scoop up a tiny bit of amethyst the looters had somehow missed. Caressing it as if 'twere a diamond, I placed the stone in my pocket.

Our dried herbs had been torn from the walls and trampled beneath booted feet. Not a stick of furniture nor even the braided rugs that had covered the floors remained, and I knew without checking the shed that the horse had been taken as well. They'd left nothing untouched.

I went to the hearth though, tugging at the smooth round stones until I found the very large one that came free at my touch. And then I set it aside and reached into the hole it left. There was a cloth bag there, stuffed full. Frowning, I pulled the bag out and sat down on the floor, untying its drawstring and looking inside. There was a smaller pouch within its folds, a pouch I found to be heavy with coin. And a dark, hooded cloak, lined with fur, all rolled up tight to make it fit in the bag. And there was a book. A beautiful leather-bound grimoire, filled with page upon page of my mother's delicate script.

I opened the cover and saw a necklace, a golden pentacle, with a cradle moon adorning one curve of its circle and the beautiful image of a goddess reclining in the moon's embrace. I lifted the pendant and beneath it, on the page, saw a note just for me.

*My dearest Raven,*

*If you are reading this, you are on your own now. Do not mourn me, child. If my lifetime ended, 'twas only because it had served its purpose, and now I will go on to another. But for you, child, 'tis only the beginning.*

*Wear the pentacle, for it holds all the magic I ever possessed. My strength and my wisdom are within it, and they are yours to call upon so long as you wear it. But keep it near your heart, and not out for the world to see. 'Twas never mine to wear. I only held it in trust for you. It marks you as who and what you are.*

*In this book are all the secrets I've learned. But the one I will tell you now is the most important of all of them. My daughter, my beloved Raven, you are not like me. And the path before you will not be an easy one.*

*Raven St. James, you are an immortal witch, a High Witch, though you've never known such beings existed.*

*When you suffer and die for the first time, you will know that what I say is true, for within a short while your body will revive itself. And from that moment on you will be stronger than before, and will never grow older.*

*I know this must shock you. But you are not the only one. There are others like you, though their numbers are few. And not all of them are good and pure of heart, as I know you to be.*

*The stories of them have been handed down through the generations of my family, and I will tell you all I know, and hope you put the knowledge to good use, to keep you safe. But I fear there is much I do not know, Raven. Things you will have to learn on your own.*

*There are two kinds of immortal witches. The dark, and the light. The evil, and the good.*

*In some previous lifetime, my daughter, you died while attempting to save the life of another witch. Because of this, you were born into this lifetime with the gift of immortality. But this is only one of two ways that gift can be passed on.*

*The other way is far more sinister. By taking the life of an immortal witch, one also takes that witch's immortality, indeed, all of her power. I can imagine you crooking your delicate brow as you read this, wondering how one can kill someone who is immortal. There is but a single way, child. And that is to take the witch's heart from her very breast, and to lock it up in a small box where it will go on beating forever. Whoever retains the box, retains the power. Witches created in this way are dangerous to you, Raven, for they are never content with the power they have acquired. They cannot be, for eventually, the captive heart will weaken, its life force drained by the dark one who took it. The Dark Witch begins to weaken, to grow pale and sickly just as any mortal suffering from the ravages of old age might do. And so the witch must kill again and again, in order to survive.*

*Always beware of others like you, Raven. For you'll have no way of knowing whether they be dark or light. You will recognize them as Immortals, however, by the necklace many of them wear, one such as the one I give you now, and by the first touch of their hand. I do not know how or why that is, but I know 'tis true. Be careful, my love. Let no Dark Witch take your heart.*

*Hidden in the center of this book is a dagger that has been handed down through the generations of my family from time immemorial, just as this pendant was, to be held for the day when a special one was born to us. 'Tis as if they knew, somehow. 'Tis yours, Raven, meant for you all along, I am certain. Keep it with you always and learn to wield it with skill. You will need to defend yourself from attack by those others. Above all, child, trust no one.*

*No one.*

*And know that wherever you are and for as long as forever, my love remains with you. Always with you.*

*Your loving mother, Lily St. James*

Blinking in shock at all I had read, I let the book fall open to its center and saw a jewel-encrusted dagger, tucked inside its sheath and hidden by the clever way my mother had cut away the centers of some of the pages. I took the weapon in my hands, turned it slowly, felt its weight, and tried to imagine myself using such a tool to do harm to another living being. The thought made me shiver. I did not believe I could ever do it.

But there was more to try to understand. More, so much that my mind could barely comprehend the enormity of it.

"Immortal," I whispered. And I knew, I already knew, 'twas the truth.

# ALSO BY MAGGIE SHAYNE

## SMALL-TOWN CONTEMPORARY SERIES

The Texas Brand

The Oklahoma Brands

The McIntyre Men

The Texas Brand: Generations

## THRILLERS & ROMANTIC SUSPENSE SERIES

Brown and de Luca Return

The Fatal series

Shattered Sisters

Danger After Dawn

## PARANORMAL ROMANCE

The Portal

Wings in the Night

The Immortals

By Magic

# ABOUT THE AUTHOR

New York Times bestselling author Maggie Shayne has published more than 60 novels and 23 novellas. She has written for 7 publishers and 2 soap operas, and is a 15-time RITA® Award nominee and a RITA® winner.

Maggie lives in a beautiful, century-old, happily haunted farmhouse named "Serenity" in the wildest wilds of Cortland County, NY, with her husband and soul mate, Lance. Maggie is a Wiccan high priestess, legal clergy, and an avid follower and coach of the Law of Attraction